CLOSEST PLACE TO HEAVEN

Kezia McCoy had had a crush on Shann Evans for years, and it was a shock when she was forced to realise just how much she had been wasting her time. She had fallen in love with one man who didn't take her seriously— and she wasn't going to make the same mistake twice . . .

CLOSEST PLACE TO HEAVEN

BY

LYNSEY STEVENS

MILLS & BOON LIMITED
15–16 BROOK'S MEWS
LONDON W1A LDR

First published 1983
Australian copyright 1983
Philippine copyright 1983
This edition 1983

© Lynsey Stevens 1983

ISBN 0 263 74239 3

Set in Monophoto Plantin 10 on 11½ pt.
01–0583 – 50787

Made and printed in Great Britain by Richard Clay (The Chaucer Press) Ltd, Bungay, Suffolk

For
Zena and Thea,
two of Norfolk Island's
kind and friendly hearts.

CHAPTER ONE

A PAIR of brown hand-tooled leather shoes made a soft crunching sound on the cement floor of the workshop and Kezia turned her head towards the noise, catching sight of the shoes and about a foot of dark brown slacks. Wiping an overall-clad arm across her damp brow, she bit off an angry exclamation as her hand clutching a ring spanner, came into contact with a metal cross member, grazing her knuckles. A frown puckered her forehead as she sighed exasperatedly. The brown shoes had paused at the sound of her movements and she addressed the owner of the feet from her position on her back beneath the small blue car.

'Shann! Thank goodness. You can give me a hand,' she said with a measure of relief. 'I've been seething for the past hour, to put it mildly. When I get hold of that wretched brother of mine I'm going to wring his neck, and that's for sure!'

The brown shoes took a couple of steps towards the car.

'He took Toby fishing and he promised he'd be back in time to do this,' she continued, 'but as usual he's conspicuous by his absence. You'd think after twenty years I'd have learned, wouldn't you? Well, no amount of fish are going to talk his way out of it this time. I'll ... I'll ...' she searched for a torture to fit the crime. 'Well, I'll think of something.'

Her eyes turned back to the shoes. 'Look, be a pal,

7

will you, and hop in and pump the brakes for me,' she asked as she fitted the spanner back on the bleeder screw and ensured that the piece of transparent plastic tube she'd pushed on to the screw was buried in the brake fluid in the bottle standing on the floor beside her.

The car moved as Shann climbed into the driver's seat.

'Okay,' she called. 'Pedal down. Up. Down.' She adjusted the screw with the ease of much practice. 'How's that?'

'Seems fine,' came the muffled answer from above.

'Right. Now for the driver's side.' She levered herself over to the other wheel and repeated the process before sliding out from beneath the car. Bending over, she collected the tools she'd been using and as she began to replace everything angrily on the bench she frowned again, turning as the door of the car was closed quietly, although her assistant was still hidden behind the upraised bonnet.

'Honestly, Shann, I've had Chris lately! He's supposed to be in charge of all this.' She waved the spanner she still clutched rather dangerously, almost knocking the bottle of brake fluid she'd placed on the bench, glancing at it accusingly as she set it in a safer position to the back closer to the wall.

'And don't you go spilling all over everything,' she told the offending bottle, 'or that would be the very last straw!'

She began to turn back towards the car. 'I ask you, Shann, am I a mechanic or a . . .?' Her voice died away as her eyes told her she was not addressing Shannon Evans as she surmised she was. 'Oh, I'm so sorry.' The words were having trouble squeezing out from her suddenly numb vocal chords and constricted throat and she knew a red stain had crept into her cheeks.

The stranger was taller than Shann and possibly broader in the shoulders. His hair was dark but not as black as Shann's and he had the most vividly blue eyes she had ever seen, incongruous with his hair colour. And he was really attractive . . .

Suddenly feeling she might have been gaping open-mouthed at him, she took a gulping breath, her cheeks burning again. 'I thought you were a friend of mine,' she said by way of explanation, her voice not quite her own. 'Can I help you?' Her eyes went to the door which led through to the office in the centre of the shopping area on Taylor's Road.

His smile drove interesting creases on either side of his mouth below his high cheekbones and his compelling blue eyes crinkled at the corners. For some inexplicable reason Kezia's legs wobbled weakly and a strange feeling teased the pit of her stomach.

'I was looking to book a tour of the island.' His voice was deep and resonant, and flowed silkily over her ears. 'But there doesn't seem to be anyone out in the office.' He motioned towards the door.

'Oh.' Kezia blinked, his voice causing her even more discomposure, and she flushed again, drawing on what self-possession she had left to muster. 'I . . . Just a moment and I'll take you through. My mother must have stepped out for a while.'

She pulled at the top studs of the oversized overalls she was wearing which she'd borrowed from her brother. And just as quickly she stopped. Somehow she didn't want to step out of the overalls in front of this man, although she knew she was fully dressed in shirt and shorts beneath them, and she chastised herself angrily. There was no reason why she shouldn't act as naturally with this man as she did with any other tourist. After all, her family was in the tourist business and she was used to all manner of different people. Yes, male tourists as well, as she told herself. Thin. Fat. Short. Tall, like this one. Her eyes flicked furtively over him. Very tall. Broad, muscular and obviously physically fit.

Pulling a piece of rag from her pocket, she gave her greasy fingers a wipe, wrinkling her nose at the state of her hands. He moved then, towards her, and one strong hand reached out for her cleaning cloth.

'May I?' he asked, his face alight with amusement. His other hand held her chin steady while he rubbed gently at two dark smears, one above her eyebrow and one along her small slightly upturned nose. He gave her nose another rub and her eyes opened widely to meet his at least a foot above hers, her heartbeats racing in her chest.

'They're freckles,' she said huskily, her voice tight after the shiver his fingers had brought to her body had subsided.

A stillness seemed to hold him and the air between them all but crackled.

'Kez! Kezia! How's the Charade coming?' A voice from the outer office cut between them, severing the circle of heightened awareness that had been spun about them.

'The sun's kisses,' the man said softly, touching her nose gently with one finger before he turned and tossed the rag on to the bench behind them.

'Kez!' A petite dark-haired woman, who could easily have been mistaken for Kezia's older sister, stopped in surprise in the doorway. 'Oh. Good afternoon,' she smiled, her eyes going to her daughter and then back to the tall man.

He inclined his head.

'Mum, this gentleman would like to enquire about our tours,' Kezia put in quickly, her hand going rather uncharacteristically to smooth her dark brown curls.

'Of course. I'm sorry I wasn't at my post when you came in,' Kezia's mother smiled. 'I'd probably just stepped out to give some directions to an American couple. I'm Allie McCoy, by the way. Please come through.' She turned to lead the tall man into the office and then paused to glance back at her daughter. 'The Martins are here for the car,' she said softly, indicating the blue Charade with a nod of her head.

'I've just finished. I'll bring it around front,' Kezia replied, and waited until she was alone before slipping out of the none-too-clean overalls and crossing to the car. She backed it out to the petrol pump and filled the fuel tank before driving it around to the front of the office where a middle-aged couple were waiting to collect the little blue car.

When she had seen them on their way Kezia walked into the office to join her mother, who sat once more at her desk, and she very casually ran her eyes down the open tour bookings folder, finding the name on the bottom of the list. B. Devereaux, Cascade Court. So he was staying at Shannon Evans' motel. Maybe she'd see him when . . .

'He was a nice fellow.' Her mother's words cut in on her thoughts and Kezia looked up quickly.

'Who was?' she asked innocently.

Allie McCoy smiled gaily, making her look far too young to have a twenty-year-old daughter, let alone a twenty-three-year-old son. 'The man you were talking to in the workshop. Mr Devereaux.'

'Oh, him. Yes. He was all right.' Kezia picked up the other folder which contained the bookings for the half-day tour, giving it an equal amount of attention.

'He's from Brisbane,' continued her mother.

'Mmm,' murmured Kezia noncommittally.

'He arrived yesterday and he's taking the full day tour tomorrow. Pity it wasn't your turn for the full day tour,' she added, her eyes twinkling. 'He's so handsome.'

Kezia raised her eyebrows. 'Are you trying to matchmake, Mum?'

'Well, he is the nicest-looking mainlander I've seen in ages,' smiled her mother teasingly.

'You've just said the operative word—mainlander. And apart from that you know I'm not interested,' she finished strongly, a fleeting thought that she appeared to be protesting just a little too strongly crossing her mind. 'Besides, he's probably got a nice wife and a couple of lovely kids waiting at home in Brisbane.'

'He didn't look married,' began Mrs McCoy.

'As handsome as he is——' Kezia began, and pulled a face at her mother's triumphant smile. 'As handsome as you say he is,' she amended, 'I can't see him being left on the shelf. Some fast lady will have snapped him up years ago. I'll bet he's over thirty.'

'And that's so ancient, isn't it?' laughed her mother. 'I can feel the grey hairs multiplying in my forty-year-old hair!'

'Oh, Mum, don't tease!' Kezia laughed. 'You know you don't look a day over thirty.'

'Then perhaps I should be taking that tour tomorrow,' Allie said with mock seriousness, breaking into a delighted laugh at the momentary shock on her daughter's face. 'I'm only joking, love.'

Just then two figures entered the office, both shirtless and wearing salt-stained shorts, white teeth flashing in their tanned faces. That they were brothers couldn't be doubted, and, although the older one was a good two inches taller, there was a distinct family resemblance in their features and both had dark curly hair, the same shade as Kezia's.

'Chris McCoy! Just the person I wanted to see!' Kezia drew herself up to her full five feet four inches. 'I've got a bone to pick with you.'

'Oho! Duck, brother! Little sister's on the warpath,' grinned Chris, shoving his young brother between himself and Kezia.

'Warpath! Is it any wonder? You said, in fact you promised you'd be back in time to service the three cars out back, but what happens? There am I, grease from stem to stern and my fingernails will take ages to recover, while you enjoy a relaxing morning fishing!' She paused to draw breath.

'Isn't she beautiful when she's mad?' Chris put in. 'Her eyes go all black and flashy.'

The younger boy bit off a laugh, covering his mouth with his hand.

'I'm serious, Chris.' Kezia dragged an angry breath.

'And I'm sorry, Kez. It was Toby's fault. He found a spot where the fish were really biting, so we couldn't just up tacks and leave.' He raised his hands and let them fall. 'We sold our catch down at the restaurant and we saved a couple for dinner tonight, didn't we, mate?'

'That's the truth, Kez,' nodded Toby, opening his fishing creel to display four large trumpeters. 'They're beauties, Mum. Look! The biggest I've caught this holidays.' He turned a beguiling smile on his older sister. 'Don't be too hard on Chris, I really did hold him up.'

'Yes, and I can see the bruise where you twisted his arm,' replied Kezia drily. 'Well, I'm still not happy about having to do those cars. They're your job, Chris. And on top of that the Charade needed the brakes adjusting, and you know I hate doing that on my own.'

'What can I say, Kez?' Chris smiled sheepishly at her. 'Except you're the best sister a bloke could have.'

'Oh, yes,' she said sarcastically, and glanced at her wristwatch. 'I *was* going swimming.'

'There's still time, isn't there?' Chris lifted her arm so that he could look at her watch, too. 'We might come with you, seeing as you've finished the cars.'

Kezia's mouth opened and he put a brotherly arm about her shoulders. 'If I've said it once I've said it a hundred times, Sis—you're worth at least half a dozen guys. Maybe we should give her a rise, Mum.'

'Maybe we should give me your wages you mean,' said Kezia, and walked across to the door. 'I might ring the motel and see if Shann would like to come down to the beach with me.'

She didn't see the quick look her brother exchanged with their mother.

'He's not at the motel,' said Chris, and Kezia stopped and turned back to face him.

'Isn't he? When did you see him?'

'His car was parked outside the Leagues Club when we came past,' said her brother, finding an interest in the paperweight he'd lifted from his mother's desk.

'Oh. Maybe they've got darts team practice,' she said thoughtfully. 'I might call in on my way home. Want me to take the fish with me?'

'That might be a good idea,' said her mother, no smile on her face now. 'I'll be home about five-thirty—I want to pick up a few groceries on my way.'

'Okay.' Kezia went outside to her small motorbike and strapped the creel on the back before heading off towards the Leagues Club.

She slowed down as she passed the single-storey building, but Shann's distinctive yellow Alfa Romeo wasn't among the cars outside, so she continued on home, changing into her bikini and slipping back into her shorts and top before heading towards Kingston and the beach.

When she reached the junction of Taylor's Road and Queen Elizabeth Avenue, on an impulse she took the latter fork and headed for the Cascade Court Motel. It wasn't far out of her way and maybe Shann would join her in a swim. She hadn't seen him for over a week. He seemed so busy these days.

Cascade Court was a large hotel-motel complex tucked away behind a lavishness of tropical gardens and shrubbery. Sturdy and distinctive Norfolk pines shielded the buildings from the road and only the white cement posts with a sedate sign saying 'Cascade Court' gave any inkling of what lay beyond.

The short driveway was flanked by profusely flowering hibiscus in shades of reds and yellows, and the well tended lawns were dotted with beds of begonias and day-lilies. The main covered entrance-way was in an imposing double-storey building while the rest of the motel ran back, single-storied, in a V-shape with more gardens and a large pool and open barbecue area between the two blocks of rooms.

It was one of the largest resorts on the island, containing some sixty self-contained rooms, besides having its own licensed restaurant, three bars and various other entertainment rooms, and had been built by Shannon Evans' father and grandfather. Since his father's death three years earlier, Shann had run the whole outfit himself.

Leaving her motorcycle parked at the side of the driveway beside Shann's Alfa, Kezia ran up the few steps into the plush foyer, casting her eyes about for Shann's tall figure. The reception desk was unattended, so she strode along the short thickly carpeted hallway off to the right that led to Shann's office, pausing before the partly open office doorway, wondering if she should continue past and up the staircase to Shann's living quarters on the next floor.

However, the sound of voices from behind the half open door had her stepping inside the office. Raewyn Bourke, Shann's secretary-receptionist, was seated at her desk, her typewriter in front of her, and Shann was leaning towards her talking quietly and earnestly, his face frowning his ill-humour.

'Well, I can't abide him myself, but it's a case of having to put up with him, I'm afraid.' He grimaced. 'That's why I'm depending on you to soap him up a bit for me, flash those beautiful green eyes at him.'

'But, Shann . . .' the girl began.

'I know, I know. I feel a heel asking you, darling, but——' he stopped and shrugged. 'It's a means to an end, if you see my point.' He pursed his lips with irritation. 'What gets my goat is that the bastard's so sure of . . .' He broke off as he caught Kezia's movement. 'Hell! It's you, Kezia.' He stood up with what seemed like a sigh of relief, exchanging a quick look with the woman at the desk. 'Don't mind us, we've had a bad day.'

'Hi! You two do look hard at work.' Kezia smiled at them. 'There's no one on duty outside.'

'Oh, for heaven's sake!' A slight colour had flushed Shann's cheeks and he shifted irritably on his feet. 'That girl will have to go, Rae.'

'I'll go and check on it.' Raewyn Bourke stood up, or rather, uncoiled herself, thought Kezia.

She was tall, cool and poised, a New Zealander by birth, and she had been working for Shann for the past two years. Kezia always thought she should have been a model rather than a receptionist, and wondered once again what kept such an attractive woman on the island when she could have earned so much more lucrative wages on the mainland. She shrugged to herself. Perhaps Raewyn simply liked the peace and quiet of this South Pacific haven. Somehow, Kezia always felt young and naïve and very much at a disadvantage when Raewyn was around, and she couldn't have been more than a few years older than Kezia herself.

'What's your problem, Kezia?' Shann was asking, his hands gathering together some typewritten sheets. His eyes had followed the other girl's departure before turning back to Kezia.

'No problems. I just thought you might like a swim. I'm on my way down to the beach now.' She felt slightly puzzled as his eyes didn't quite meet hers.

'Sorry, love, I'm up to my ears, and have been all day.' He leant back against the desk, his long legs thrust out before him, and Kezia remembered the other long legs she had mistaken for Shann's a little earlier and her eyes moved over his familiar figure.

Shannon Evans was the island's most eligible bachelor and, at twenty-six, he had had years of experience when it came to dealing with the hopeful young ladies of the district. He had certainly taken quite a few of them out, but none of them had succeeded in tying him down. As he was a friend of her brother's he had probably spent more time with Kezia than with any other girl on the island, a fact that gave her a thrill of pleasure as she stood looking at him.

He was a handsome young man, just on six foot tall, with thick straight dark hair that he wore a little long, he sported a very 'in vogue' moustache, and in his dark slacks and Polynesian print tailored shirt he had reason to be pleased with his lot.

'You must have been busy lately. I haven't seen you in ages,' she said, suddenly remembering Chris had said he'd seen Shann at the Leagues Club. Obviously Chris had been mistaken, or maybe someone had borrowed Shann's car.

Shann gave her a crooked grin. 'Don't tell me you've missed me?' He leant over and ruffled her dark curls, and she frowned.

'I'm not a baby, Shann,' she said sharply, and drew herself up to her full height with some dignity.

His eyes moved down to her breasts, moulded by her thin top, and he smiled again. 'No, you're sure not a baby. In fact, you've grown up some while I haven't been watching.'

'I've been grown up for years.' She felt a little breathless at the light in his dark eyes and knew she was blushing. 'I'm twenty now.'

'But you still blush very prettily,' he teased, and drew her forward, putting his lips on hers.

It wasn't a long kiss and she felt vaguely dissatisfied, and as he went to move away she slid her arms around his waist and moved closer to him. If he hadn't taken her by surprise she could have kissed him back, showed him how much he meant to her.

'If I'm so grown up surely you could give me a grown-up kiss,' she said quietly, part of her horrified at her audaciousness.

Shann was momentarily taken aback, then he gave a quick laugh. 'Well, well! You are growing up in leaps and bounds, aren't you, Kez?' His eyes moved over her again with a thoroughness that she wasn't sure she liked before his lips descended to claim hers, his arms pulling her hard against his body.

Kezia had never had time or inclination for fooling around with boys her own age, and this was the first time she had felt the hardness of a masculine body against her. When Shann released her and stood back she blinked up at him, her eyes round with shocked surprise. His kiss hadn't been unpleasant exactly, but it left her with a slight disappointment. Somehow she had expected more than just a pleasantness . . .

A slight cough from the open doorway had her starting guiltily backwards and they both swung around towards the sound. An embarrassed flush rushed over Kezia's cheeks as her eyes met a pair of vivid blue ones that held a faint hint of mockery. How long had he been standing there?

'I beg your pardon, Evans.' The deep voice was as fluid as she remembered it and it caused the same teasing flutter in the pit of her stomach. 'I didn't realise you were occupied.'

Had she just imagined the slight pause before that last word?

'No—no!' Shann was overly jovial. 'What can I do for you, Devereaux?'

Kezia's eyes moved back to Shann, trying to disguise her surprise at the deference in his tone. Whoever the stranger was Shann was pulling out all stops to impress. B. Devereaux. Her eyes went back to him. She was sure she hadn't heard of him.

'I was thinking of a swim, salt water rather than the pool, and wondered if you could recommend the best place.' He wore a pair of dark blue denim shorts that hung low on his hips, hugging his tanned muscular thighs, and a pale blue T-shirt that clung to his broad shoulders like a second skin. He shifted the large beach towel he carried and slung it over his shoulder, the thin material of his shirt not disguising the play of his muscles.

'Sure,' smiled Shann with genial bonhomie. 'Just the afternoon for swimming.' He turned and drew Kezia forward. 'As a matter of fact young Kezia here is just off to Emily Bay. She'll drive you down, won't you, Kez?'

'Oh, I . . .' Kezia began, for some reason absolutely horrified at the thought of spending time with this particular tall dark Australian, alone. She gulped. 'I'm on my motorbike. I didn't bring the car,' she blurted out, barely masking her relief.

'I've ridden a bike before,' smiled the other man. 'I don't mind going pillion—if you've no objection to taking me with you, that is.' One dark eyebrow rose, his blue eyes challenging her.

'Of course she doesn't mind, do you, Kezia? I know, I'll lend you my car for the afternoon.'

'But suppose you need it yourself?' She turned to him, her eyes slightly imploring, wondering why Shann was bending over backwards so far to please this man.

'I won't be needing it—I'll be tied up here for hours yet,' laughed Shann. 'Well, that's sorted out.' He took hold of her arm and moved her towards the door, his eyes not meeting hers. 'Heck, I haven't introduced you two.'

'Miss McCoy and I have already met,' said the other man, and Shann's eyes went from one to the other enquiringly. 'I booked a tour for tomorrow with her mother,' he explained.

'I see. You'll enjoy that. Well, that's it, then.' Shann picked up Kezia's hand and put the keys to his car into it. 'I hope you enjoy your swim. I'd really love to join you, but,' he shrugged, 'that's how it goes. Some of us have to keep things going.'

The telephone rang at the reception desk as they crossed to the main entrance, and Raewyn's eyes watched them as she answered the phone and motioned to Shann that the call was for him. He apologetically excused himself and left them to walk out to the car together.

Kezia's legs were carrying her along, but she wasn't quite sure how they were managing it. Shann had left them before she could make any objection to the situation and she now found herself with Shann's car keys in one hand and the enigmatic and disturbing Mr Devereaux beside her.

'You know, I can call a taxi if you'd rather not take me,' he said, and she looked up quickly, all of a sudden worried that her reticence had appeared rude.

A mixture of emotions churned over inside her. He was unsmiling now, his face set and expressionless, his blue eyes veiled by his thick dark lashes.

'Oh, no, I don't mind,' she hastened to placate him and his lips thinned a little. 'I . . .' She made an attempt at a smile. 'If you did call a taxi I'd most probably have to drive you anyway. We have the twenty-four-hour taxi service as well, you see,' she finished with wry amusement.

His eyes held hers for a moment before he spoke. 'You don't seem to be able to shake me off, do you?' he said softly.

CHAPTER TWO

AND his eyes remained on her face unwaveringly for a heartstopping moment before he gave a soft chuckle, a deep sound that vibrated through her, making her swallow nervously at the entirely new sensations he was awakening within her. Then the corners of his lips lifted into a smile like the one he'd given her in the workshop earlier, and this time it seemed to have an even more devastating effect on her.

She forced her rubbery legs to move, walking around to the driver's side of the Alfa, anything to put some distance between them so she could catch her faltering breath.

'The door's open. We don't need to lock up on the island,' she said somewhat hoarsely.

But in the confines of the car it was much worse. He was far too close and her eyes had a tendency to slide sideways of their own will, taking in his tanned bare legs, running erotically down to his thrust-out sandalled feet.

Good grief! What was wrong with her? It wasn't as though she was unused to ferrying strangers around the island. She did it almost every day of the week. And some of them were no less handsome in their own way than the man in the seat beside her. This would have to stop right now.

Chastising herself severely, she started the engine and backed quickly around in a smoothly executed three-point turn and headed back down the driveway to the road.

'Not a bad little car,' he said evenly as she searched desperately for something to say to broach the heavy heightened silence.

'Yes. Shann bought it last year when he was in Sydney. He's very proud of it.' Kezia had relaxed just a little at his easy tone. Obviously, he was unaware of her discomfort, and for that she was profoundly grateful. He probably . . .

'I'm surprised he lets you drive it,' he spoke across her thoughts and his words had her hackles rising angrily.

'He knows he can trust me with it,' she replied through clenched teeth. 'Besides, I've been driving for years.' She shot a quick glance at him and saw his lips twitch with mirth. 'We're allowed to ride motorcycles at fifteen here. From daylight till dusk,' she added with reluctant honesty. 'Anyway,' she shrugged, 'Shann should have confidence in me. He taught me to drive, after all.'

'That explains his confidence, then,' he said, and she wondered if she was imagining the thread of amusement in his tone again.

With cool precision she changed down a gear and turned into Rooty Hill Road. 'If you look to your left you'll get a spectacular view of the beach where we're going.' She changed the subject, slipping unconsciously into her best tourist guide voice, telling herself that would put a respectable and relaxing distance between them. 'Would you like me to pull over?'

'Please,' he said, and when she stopped he climbed out of the car and stood gazing at the panorama below.

Slowly Kezia joined him, thinking she could hardly

stay in the car. They weren't terribly high up, but from their elevated viewpoint the coastline and the Pacific Ocean swept before them, more colourful in their naturalness than a picture postcard.

'Beautiful,' the man Devereaux remarked, almost to himself, and then eventually turned to Kezia, who stood watching him through her lashes, her dark curls tossing about in the stiff breeze. 'Beautiful,' he repeated softly.

The wind was also lifting his dark hair back from his forehead and she let her lash-shielded eyes move over his strong profile. Very attractive, she thought. Slightly curved dark eyebrows; straight nose; high cheekbones; strongly defined lips, the lower full and hinting sensuality; square jaw; firm chin and the solid powerful column of his throat. Too attractive! And very sure of that attraction.

'That little stretch of beach is where we're headed?' he asked, indicating the curve of the turquoise green sand-fringed inlet skirted by the dark green of Norfolk pines.

'Yes. Emily Bay.'

'The colours of the water are incredible.' He half turned towards her, his eyes going back to the view. 'But I suppose you're used to it, living here.'

'Oh, no, I never tire of it. Especially this view. It's my second favourite place on the island.' She sighed, her eyes shiningly following his. 'I love it.' She took a deep breath of the clean clear salty air and then realised his blue eyes were watching her.

'I can see you do,' was all he said, his eyes falling downwards over her slender body, her clothes moulded to her shape by the wind, before he turned back to the scene below.

'The islands,' he pointed, 'they're radically different in colour.'

Kezia nodded. 'The smaller one is Nepean. It's limestone and has an area of about ten acres and rises over a hundred feet,' she told him.

'And the larger one is Philip Island?'

'Yes. And it's volcanic. It rises about nine hundred feet and is a mile and a quarter long. I'm afraid the vegetation has suffered from man and animals. Although there's still a few pines on the island most of the plant life has been eaten by pigs, goats and rabbits. The severe erosion is responsible for the strange colours. But both islands are breeding places for seabirds—gannets, petrels and noddies. And around on Point Ross and Point Howe we even have nesting muttonbirds.' He was watching her again and her voice died away a little selfconsciously. 'I'm sorry.' She shrugged. 'Once a tour guide always a tour guide!'

'I appreciate having you sharing your local knowledge, and I assure you I am interested, Kezia.' His deep voice turned her name into a soft melody, taken with the rest of his words by the wind and her eyes went involuntarily to his.

Their blueness was accentuated by reflections from the sky around him and he held her with the intensity of his expression. Her heart was fluttering, then began to hammer in her head to echo with his quietly spoken words. 'I am interested, Kezia.' And she had a feeling, part anticipatory excitement, part reluctant trepidation, that he wasn't only talking about the history of the island, that she now stood before an unknown path, its direction a shrouded challenge.

With a superhuman effort her eyes broke from the compelling hold of his and she escaped to the car, sitting with her fingers locked around the steering wheel to still their shaking as she waited for him to rejoin her. A faint feeling of cowardice forced its way into her mind and she couldn't thrust it away. She swallowed agitatedly. She wasn't ready, wasn't prepared to set foot on the path down which he was offering to lead her—and, what was more, this man was a stranger. If anyone was to lead her anywhere she wanted it to be Shann. She had adored him for as long as she could remember.

The stranger remained looking at the scene below for a few moments more before turning back to the car, and Kezia drove on in silence until the ruins, some partially restored, came into view.

'Kingston,' he said, a question and a statement.

'Yes. Originally the settlement was known as Sydney, but it was later changed to Kings Town to avoid confusion with the Sydney on the mainland. Kingston evolved from that.' Turning the car left, she drove slowly pointing out the row of cottages, a couple still to be restored, on the high side of the road. 'This is Quality Row, Kingston's main street.' Just past the cottages she made a U-turn and headed back along Quality Row again.

Cattle, looking well fed and contented, grazed by the roadside and chickens and geese roamed the low ground between Quality Row and the prison ruins.

They lost sight of the sea for a short time as they drove behind sand dunes, grass-covered, with the vine-growing violet morning glories adding their special splash of colour, but the sea appeared again as Kezia turned alongside the golf course, its greens fenced to deter the grazing cattle. She pulled the Alfa to a halt beneath the shade of a tree and glanced quickly at her passenger, to find him taking in the length of the Kingston coastline.

'What part of the settlement is that little building on the point there?' he asked.

'That's the Salt House. I guess it's as much a landmark as the Norfolk pines growing around it. There's also a lime kiln behind it, near the road.'

His keen eyes viewed the whole scene. And he wouldn't be missing a thing either, Kezia told herself, and climbed out of the car.

'There's changing sheds just there,' she pointed out when he'd joined her. 'So just come back here to the car when you're ready to go back to the hotel. I'll watch out for you.'

'Fine.' He strode over to the edge of the road and jumped lithely down the log retaining wall on to the sand, leaving her to stand and gaze after him, wondering again if she had been imagining the glimmer of mocking amusement in his voice before he left her.

Her eyes followed him as he walked sure-footedly down the slight incline of sand until he stopped and dropped his towel and pulled his T-shirt over his head. However, as he went to slip out of his shorts she tore her eyes away, walking irritatedly over to the side of the car before removing the shorts and top that covered her bikini. Damn the man! She'd make sure she kept the length of the beach between them, and that was for sure!

The turquoise sea was just cool and beautifully clear, and as Kezia swam and floated about she felt herself beginning to relax. There were a number of people sunbathing on the beach, islanders and tourists, and a few had called hello, but she remained alone, content with her own company.

Casting her eyes along the beach, she picked out her passenger lying on his beach towel. Obviously, he was in no hurry to leave, so she spent half an hour sunbathing herself. Sitting up, she glanced along at the car. No sign of him yet, although he had left his towel. Oh, well, she shrugged, he must be swimming. The raft moored a short distance out in the bay was deserted, so she decided to swim out to it and back to the beach before returning to the car.

She swam strongly if not with pace, and her fingers soon encountered the edge of the raft as it moved gently in the slight swell. Her hand slid over the top as she flicked her wet hair back off her face and prepared to haul herself out of the water.

Strong fingers wrapped around her wrist and with what appeared to be a minimum of effort she was out of the sea and sitting on the raft looking into those same vivid blue eyes.

'Welcome aboard, Kezia,' he laughed, brushing the wet strands of dark hair off his forehead.

The raft rocked briefly as he sat back on his haunches and Kezia could only blink at him, her eyes running over the hardness of his body, glistening with dampness. Droplets of salty moisture shone like precious stones in the sunlight as, drop by drop, they ran off his broad tanned shoulders.

No unfit, sedentary type, this one, she thought as her eyes slid downwards over his chest with its light mat of dark hair, his flat smooth stomach, the briefness of his dark blue swimming trunks and the flexed muscles of his thighs as he balanced himself on the unsteady raft.

'Do I pass the physical?' he asked softly, and Kezia felt a flush of shame wash up over her neck and face.

Had she been staring so openly at him? Of course she had. Like a lovesick teenager who hadn't seen a man's body before. She cringed. He must think her so naïve!

He lent forward, his knees resting on the decking and his hand came up to hold her head, his fingers tingling the skin at her nape. 'I sure hope so, Kezia,' he murmured huskily, the glimmer of humour gone from his face. 'Because you most definitely pass mine.' His dark head blotted out the sun as his lips came down to claim hers.

In those first few seconds, minutes, hours, Kezia could only let his lips caress hers as surprise held her motionless. But then a sudden yearning began to gather momentum deep within her, rising to dictate her reaction. She was kissing him back before she even knew she was and his other hand moved sensuously up her bare arm to rest against her neck, his thumb brushing along the line of her jaw, now finding the sensitive pulse at the base of her throat. She moaned softly, leaning closer, her body demanding a response while her mind spun crazily, not crediting what was happening.

Her hands went out to the solidness of his chest her fingertips luxuriating in the damp dark curls, registering the acceleration of his heartbeats as his kiss deepened, plundering, igniting a smouldering glow inside her that burst into a shower of sensual sparks.

It was pure pleasure, this heady sensation he was creating, and she simply gave herself up to the reeling enjoyment of that unfamiliar pleasure. This was just as she'd imagined being kissed would be. And more. So very much more. Her hands slid upwards to his silky damp shoulders, thrilling to the muscular strength beneath his tanned skin.

They could have been the only two people on earth as far as Kezia was concerned, two people in a world of their own, the raft adrift in the blue Pacific, the sandy beach, the fringing shore of a deserted tropical atoll. But the beach wasn't deserted. The thought fought its way through the mists of hazy euphoria. They were in full view of everyone and lots of those people on the beach knew her and knew her well. And they knew Shann.

'No—please!' She pushed against his body, knowing self-derisively that her 'please' had no substance of command, that it was more like a sensuous invitation.

This was all wrong. She shouldn't be kissing him like this, this stranger. It should be Shann. She'd loved him for as long as she could remember. It was Shann she wanted to kiss with this burning fervour, this all-consuming desire. When she'd kissed Shann that afternoon she now recognised that this had been what she'd expected to feel. But she hadn't. Warning bells were clanging loudly.

'No!' The word burst from her as she churned with uncertainty.

He moved slightly away, his hands still holding her, his eyes half closed as he looked down at her. 'No?' He raised one eyebrow, a trace of irony in his voice.

'I . . . No. You shouldn't be kissing me like that. It's not . . .' Her hand went to her swollen lips and then fell away.

His eyes probed hers and one corner of his mouth lifted in a crooked smile that tugged at her heart strings. 'You asked me for it, Kezia.' His voice was soft and full of an emotion that had her blood pounding in her veins.

'Asked you? I did not!' she retorted with as much dignity as her suddenly dry mouth could achieve.

'Maybe not in words,' he shrugged, 'but there are more tools than words. Your eyes asked. Your body asked.' His finger ran feather-soft over her lips and they quivered responsively. 'And your lips are still asking.'

Unable to trust herself to speak, Kezia shook her head from side to side, denying.

He smiled assuredly and nodded, affirming.

'Well, it was just . . . just . . .'

'Physical attraction?' he finished for her.

'Perhaps.' Her eyes fell from his.

'Don't knock physical attraction, Kezia.'

'I'm not!' She drew a steadying breath. 'I'm not used to——' She stopped and tried again. 'I don't make a habit of . . . of kissing strangers, and it's just that—well, Shann and I . . .' She looked up at him with a spurt of embarrassed anger tinged with defiance. 'I don't even know your name. Apart from Devereaux, that is.'

A watchfulness had tensed his body and his eyes were half closed again, shuttering his expression. 'Exactly what is Shann Evans to you?' he asked evenly.

'We're——' she paused, her eyes falling from his again. What could she say? How she wished she had the nerve to stretch the truth and say, Shann loves me as much as I love him. But she didn't know if she would be telling the truth. And she was totally unused to lying. She loved Shann, she knew she did. But how Shann really felt about her in return she just couldn't be sure. Sometimes he was so attentive and sometimes he wasn't. But he was more often than not tied up with the motel. It was such a huge responsibility resting on Shann's shoulders alone.

'I've known Shann all my life,' she said at last. 'We're the best of friends.'

His dark eyebrows rose again, sparking her anger. 'Just good friends?' he asked suggestively.

'Very good friends,' she bit out emphatically.

He lifted her left hand, feeling her ringless finger. 'Not officially?'

'No.' Kezia looked up at him. 'Not yet.'

His thumb was slowly caressing her hand and for a moment he was silent. 'Then I still have time,' he said at last.

'Time for what?' she asked, her voice higher than normal.

He smiled slowly. 'All's fair in love and war,' he said. 'And business,' he added, his smile fading a little, and Kezia frowned enquiringly.

'No matter.' He released her hand and perversely she felt a moment of regret. 'Perhaps we should be heading back. I have some phone calls to make before dinner.'

Kezia stood up with him and without a word they dived into the clear water and swam across towards the sandy beach.

They entered the motel together and Kezia looked about for Shann so she could return his car keys. Catching sight of him behind the reception desk with Raewyn Bourke, she strode across to him, a smile on her face.

'Ah, back already.' Shann's own smile was most decidedly his best. 'How was the water?'

'Great,' replied Kezia.

'Most enjoyable,' remarked a deep voice from

behind her right shoulder, making her realise he'd followed her across the foyer, and she cast a sideways glance at him.

'I knew you'd enjoy it,' laughed Shann, leaning self-assuredly on the desk.

'Thank you for taking me along, Miss McCoy.' Devereaux inclined his head, that same glimmer of amusement rife in his eyes.

'Oh, Kez doesn't mind. She'd do anything for anyone. She's a real brick.' Shann grinned at Kezia and she was again aware that he was not totally relaxed, that he was trying, for some obscure reason, to impress this stranger. In fact, he was as taut as a bowstring. And she wondered why.

'Brick?' The other man's gaze roamed over Kezia's body. 'That wouldn't be quite the word I would use,' he said quietly, his tone sending shivers down Kezia's backbone.

Shann's brown eyes went to Kezia and he laughed. 'Oh, no—right.'

What *was* all this in aid of? Kezia mused, frowning at Shann. Whatever it was, whatever game they were playing, she wasn't staying around to be sized up like a prize cow.

'By the way,' Shann was addressing the other man, 'how about joining us for dinner tonight?'

'Us?' The dark eyebrows rose enquiringly again.

'Rae and me,' replied Shann, and when those vivid blue eyes went back to Kezia he added, 'Oh, and Kezia, too, if she can make it.'

'Oh, I don't . . .' she began, flushing slightly that she had been an afterthought on Shann's part.

'Of course you can come.' Shann's voice overrode hers. 'You haven't anything on, have you?'

'No, but . . .'

'That settles it, then. Three's an uneven number anyway.' Shann rubbed his hands together in an uncharacteristically nervous gesture. 'How does eight o'clock sound?' he asked the other man.

'Fine. I'll look forward to it.'

Picking up her light crocheted lace shawl, Kezia went into the living-room to wait for Shann. For a reason she refused to allow herself to analyse she had decided to wear her newest dress, one she hadn't worn before, and she'd taken longer than usual over her make-up. Rarely did she ever add more than a touch of lipstick, for her tanned skin and dark-lashed eyes needed no artificial colour.

'Why, Kezia, you look lovely, dear,' her mother smiled at her as Kezia joined her.

'Thanks, Mum.' She glanced down at her dress. 'I guess there's no point in keeping this outfit for a special occasion. I thought I might as well wear it.'

'Going out to dinner with Shann isn't a special occasion?' teased her mother.

'It's not just with Shann,' she said quickly. 'Raewyn Bourke will be there too.' She adjusted the belt of her dress a little nervously. 'And that man who booked a tour with us this morning, Mr Devereaux. Remember I told you I drove him down to the beach?'

'Ah! The handsome one,' laughed Allie McCoy, and eyed her daughter's new dress knowingly. 'I knew you thought he was a dish, too.'

'Mum!' Kezia had to laugh with her mother. 'If I admit here and now that I think he's nice-looking will you stop with all this?'

'Just teasing you, love,' her mother patted her

shoulder. 'I wonder what he does for a living? He looks very distinguished, like a doctor or maybe a lawyer. Did he mention his occupation to you at the beach?'

'No. I just drove him down there. We didn't swim together.' Kezia turned away to hide the blush that lit her cheeks. They hadn't shared any conversational intimacies, but . . . 'All I know is that he's from Brisbane, and you told me that.'

'Shann will know if he's staying at Cascade Court.' Allie McCoy frowned. 'Kez, has Shann said anything to you about the motel?' she asked carefully.

'No. What about it?'

'Oh, nothing. I just wondered how things were going with him. We've hardly seen him lately, that's all. But I guess it's a full-time job.' Kezia walked over and picked up her shoulder bag. 'Well, I'm off. We should have a good time tonight. Some of the people on this afternoon's tour will be coming to the island dinner and they were an exceptionally nice group, all friends from Adelaide. Tena will love them. It's so much easier being a hostess when you have a nice group of people. 'Bye, love. Have a good time.'

'Mmm. 'Night, Mum. Say hi to Tena for me.' Kezia paced around the living-room absently moving an ornament, shifting a vase of wild roses from the bookcase to the coffee table, a frown on her face.

What could her mother have meant about Shann's motel? Surely he wasn't in financial difficulty. No, of course he wasn't, she chided herself. That was ridiculous. Cascade Court was always full or almost full no matter what time of year.

She glanced at the clock. A quarter to eight. Shann would be here any minute now.

Crossing to the mirror on the wall in the hall, she

stood on the tiptoes of her white sandals, wondering if the top of her dress wasn't just a little too low-cut. It did show the beginnings of the swell of her firm young breasts and left her shoulders bare, the bodice held in place by thin shoestring straps, a style which necessitated that she wore no bra. A tie belt of the same white material as the dress drew attention to her narrow waist, emphasising her rounded breasts and the curve of her hips. The skirt had enough fullness to glide about her legs as she walked and the plain white colour was relieved by a screen print of orange-yellow hibiscus blooms running from waist to hem to one side.

On an impulse she picked up an almost identically shaded blossom from the bowl on the hall stand and fixed it behind her ear, her dark hair curling about the flower, creating a perfect foil for its colour. She patted the bodice of the dress a little selfconsciously before chiding herself for her primness. This was the twentieth century, and after all, her bikini was far more revealing.

A car turned into the driveway and pulled up at the door, and Kezia had her hand on the screen door knob before she realised that the irregular throbbing of the engine was definitely not Shann's nicely tuned Alfa but her brother's ancient Mini-van. Really, Chris should give that poor little car a complete overhaul.

'Hello! A welcome home party!' laughed Chris as he bounded up the steps followed closely by Toby. 'Wow!' He eyed his sister as she stood beneath the hall light. 'If you weren't my bossy little sister I could go for you, babe,' he teased. 'And if you're going out looking like that I'd better come along to keep an eye on you.'

'You do look pretty great, Kez,' agreed Toby. 'Where are you going?'

'Don't tell me. Let me guess.' Chris closed his eyes and pressed a finger to his forehead. 'Out with some millionaire tourist who wants to take you away from all this?'

Toby laughed, 'Out with Shann Evans, more likely!'

'When you two comedians are quite finished,' said Kezia sternly. 'I happen to be having dinner at Cascade Court with Shann and Raewyn and one of the guests,' she told them with dignity as they followed her into the living-room. 'And Mum left your dinner on the stove. It's the fish you caught this morning,' she pursed her lips as Chris grinned sheepishly, 'so you'd better eat it now before it gets overcooked. And try to be on time for dinner in future,' she finished for good measure.

The boys saluted her before heading for the kitchen, but as he reached the doorway Chris paused to look back at his sister. 'By the way,' he said casually, 'what's this I hear about you and Shann having a right old passio on the raft at the beach?'

Kezia's face flooded with colour and Chris's teasing grin faltered. 'You mean it was you and Shann?' he asked incredulously returning to stand inside the living-room.

'Well, yes and no,' Kezia began.

'I don't believe it,' Chris frowned. 'And it's either yes or no, Kez, it can't be both?'

'Chris, what is this? I'm twenty years old, you know. If I want to kiss anyone I don't need your permission.' Kezia frowned back at him, guilt fanning her anger.

'Then it was you kissing Shann? On the raft?'

'What if it was?' She turned away, her heart skipping erratically at the remembered sensations of those cool lips moving on hers.

'Look, Kez!' Chris strode around to stand in front of her, his hands on his hips.

'For heaven's sake, Chris! What right have you got to say who I can kiss and when I can kiss? I wouldn't exactly say you were in training for a monkhood!'

'Kezia!' Chris muttered through his teeth. 'We weren't talking about me. Anyway, that's different.'

'Why? Because you're male and I'm female? I've never heard anything so biased!' She raised her hands to underscore her point.

Chris glowered at her. 'We're not going into that,' he retorted. 'All I'm saying is that I told the guy who told me he saw you on the raft, in a clinch with Shann Evans, that it wasn't you, that he must have been mistaken.' When she didn't comment he took a deep breath. 'This guy also said that the whole scene wasn't far short of being an R-rating.'

'Oh, rubbish! You know people exaggerate,' she began, turning away from him again. 'And besides that, I can't see where it's anyone's business but my own.'

'I can't believe Shann would——' Chris stopped and looked levelly at Kezia again. 'Since when has Shann been coming on strong with you, because I just might have to talk to him?'

'He hasn't. He wasn't even on the beach,' she answered, turning back to him, and could have bitten her tongue for Chris threw his head up and glared at her.

'Then who the hell was on the raft with you making like you were the only two people left on earth?' he raised his voice.

'Chris, you've got no right to ...' Her voice matched his.

'What's all the yelling about?' asked Toby, joining them, his knife and fork in one hand and his dinner in the other. 'Yours is still on the stove, Chris.'

'Keep out of this, Toby,' growled Chris, and his young brother shrugged goodnaturedly and sat down putting his plate on the coffee table in front of him and sliding Kezia's vase of roses to one side.

'Okay. You don't mind if I start without you, do you? I'm starving! And if you're going to start throwing things mind my dinner, will you?' He forked a square of tomato into his mouth, undaunted by the glares directed at him by his brother and sister.

'Well, Kezia, who was he?' pressed Chris.

Kezia gave an exasperated sigh. 'He was a guest at Cascade Court. Shann asked me to drive him to the beach. And anyway, what's wrong with a little kiss?'

'Yuck! Sloppy stuff! I thought you were above that sort of thing, Kez,' put in Toby, and found himself ignored.

'Nothing's wrong with a little kiss,' continued Chris, 'if that's all it was, but I don't think you realise just what some of these tourists are like, Kezia. Some of those guys are here simply for a plain out-and-out good time, and they don't care where or how they get it.'

'Good grief! I'm not a child, Chris,' Kezia fumed. 'I do know about the birds and the bees.'

'Hey, how about telling me all about it?' suggested Toby, his eyes wide with mock innocence.

'Shut up, Toby!' chorused Kezia and Chris.

'Kez,' Chris raised his hands and let them fall, 'what I'm trying to get across is that people aren't always what they seem. You haven't had much experience with men ... Well, you haven't,' he said firmly when his sister would have butted in. 'Most of the local guys know they'd have me to contend with if they don't treat you right and, what with the tours, you don't get much of a chance to be faced with a tourist on his own and—well, you know. Heck, Kezia, all I'm trying to say is I don't want to see you get hurt, that's all,' he finished, his ears a little pink.

'Oh, Chris!' Kezia hugged him and kissed him on the cheek, her anger forgotten.

'Favouritism! Downright favouritism!' complained Toby with a wounded look on his young face. 'How about a kiss for me? I'd tear anyone apart who looked sideways at you too, Kez. With these bare hands no less.'

Kezia gave him a playful shove. 'I'm sorry I yelled at you, Chris. I know you only meant well, but you've no need to worry about me—either of you. I've no intention of getting involved with anyone, especially a mainlander.' She wrinkled her nose. 'But thanks anyway, you're not bad brothers sometimes.'

'Well . . .' Chris looked a little embarrassed, 'you are my favourite sister when all's said and done.'

'That's not a bad achievement, Kez,' chimed in Toby. 'Favourite out of one!'

'Shove some of that food in your mouth, little brother, and spare us the mind-boggling philosophies on life,' suggested Chris, his anger gone, as he went into the kitchen for his own meal.

Five minutes later Shann's Alfa slid to a halt beside Chris's mini-van.

'There's Shann now.' Kezia grabbed her bag and

shawl, a sudden attack of butterflies gripping her stomach. 'See you both later!'

'Sure. Have fun,' said Chris with studied off-handedness.

'Hey, Kez!' Toby called after her. 'Keep away from men in case they try to lead you astray!' He gave a lecherous laugh, raised his eyebrows and twirled an imaginary moustache.

She was still laughing at him as she hurried over to Shann's car, although her smile faltered a little as a face that was becoming very familiar to her swam before her eyes. Lead her astray? Somehow she had an idea that the handsome Mr Devereaux, whatever he did for a living, wouldn't have the least bit of trouble leading any woman he fancied well and truly astray. The lady would probably be halfway there before he started!

CHAPTER THREE

'Hi, sweetie!' Shann greeted her as she slid into the passenger seat beside him. 'Sorry I'm late, I had a phone call just as I was about to leave.'

'That's okay.' Kezia smiled at him. Shann was so much safer than the stranger Devereaux and Shann was just as handsome. Well, they were two totally different men, she tried to convince herself, and then pushed the thoughts out of her mind. 'Hope the chef makes it worth waiting for.'

'Have a heart, Kez! He's the best on the island,' he replied, swinging the car around in the driveway. 'He should be—I have to pay him enough,' he added, frowning slightly.

A prickle of fear stabbed at her as she recalled her mother's words earlier, and she watched his profile as he headed back towards the motel.

'Shann, aren't things going very well at the Court?'

He laughed at her question, but she noticed he kept his eyes fixed on the road. 'Of course things are all right. Never better. Whatever gave you that idea?'

'Oh, nothing really. You just seem to be so much busier, and—well, I just wondered.'

'Don't worry your pretty head. You know the Court's the best motel on the island,' he said confidently. 'And it always will be. We're booked out pretty well solidly for the next eight weeks.'

'That's great.' Kezia sat back, reassured. 'Have you

thought any more about getting some high-standard entertainers over from the mainland?'

'I'm still tossing the scheme around,' he replied, absently. 'Plenty of time to get involved in all that.' He turned into Cascade Court and pulled up just past the entrance. 'Kez, before we go inside, can we talk a minute?' His hand went out to touch her arm as she reached for the door handle.

'Mmm.' She looked back at him questioningly, wondering why the touch of Shann's hand on her arm couldn't match the effect another hand had evoked that afternoon. She ran her eyes critically over him, telling herself he *was* handsome. She'd always thought he was the most attractive man on the island, and yet . . . 'What did you want to talk about?' she asked him evenly, refusing to listen when she told herself that only a day ago she would have been glowing with pleasure if Shann had wanted to talk to her alone.

Shann flicked a cigarette out of the packet sitting on his dashboard, lighting up before he answered her. 'How did it go at the beach this afternoon? With Devereaux, I mean?'

'Go?' Kezia frowned, a wave of guilt causing her voice to sound a shade higher than normal. 'All right. Why do you ask?'

Shann drew on his cigarette. 'Oh, nothing. I just hope it wasn't too much of a bore for you, that's all.' He shrugged. 'I guess I did kind of foist him on you. I hope I didn't spoil your afternoon.'

'No, of course you didn't. I just took him down to the beach and then drove him home. I didn't mind.' She watched him as he put the cigarette to his lips and it crossed her mind that perhaps Shann had heard about the kiss she'd shared with Devereaux just like Chris had, and he was trying to broach the subject.

Oh no! she groaned inwardly. She'd have to tell Shann that the kiss meant nothing to her, that . . . She swallowed convulsively. Lies. It was all lies. How could she tell him that the stranger's kiss meant nothing to her? She couldn't even fool herself about it, so how would she be able to convince anyone else? The truth would be written all over her face.

'What did you think of him?' Shann asked, his eyes narrowed against the smoke curling from his smouldering cigarette.

'He . . . he was quite nice.' Her voice cracked nervously, but Shann didn't seem to notice.

'He fancies you, Kezia,' Shann remarked casually, and her mouth fell open in surprise.

'Shann, don't be silly.' Her words sounded breathy to her ears and her heart had begun to pound away in her chest. 'You shouldn't joke about things like that.'

'Who said I was joking? The guy goes for you, I can tell. He watches you like a hawk. I wouldn't be a bit surprised to see him drooling.' He leaned over to stub out his cigarette.

Kezia frowned, not liking his choice of words. 'Well, I'm not interested,' she said firmly, almost convincing herself.

'And I'm glad to hear it,' he said softly, picking up her hand and holding it gently. 'Because I'm sort of used to having you around, young Kezia.'

'You know I'm always about here somewhere,' she laughed nervously, a little embarrassed by his words, although she had longed for years to hear him say something just like that. 'Part of the furniture, almost.'

'Very attractive furniture.' He paused. 'Kez, I want

to ask you a little favour.' Shann moved his thumb gently over the softness of her hand.

'Of course. What do you want me to do?' She wished he'd look at her instead of keeping his eyes fixed on the hand he held, and she wondered if he could be nervous. But Shann was always so sure of himself.

'I kind of hate myself for having to ask you to do this, but—well, Devereaux is quite an important guy in his own right and while he's here at the Court I want him kept happy, if you get my drift?'

'You mean he can influence other people into wanting to stay at Cascade Court?' She frowned slightly. 'But how can I help?'

'Just by being—well, being nice to him.'

'Nice to . . .' Kezia froze. 'Shann, just what do you mean by being nice to him?'

He looked up at her then. 'Hell, Kez! Nothing like that! I didn't mean that at all, so get that right out of your head. I simply meant if you'd give him a bit of attention tonight, charm him like I know you can, flash your big brown eyes at him, things like that.'

'Oh, Shann, I can't . . .'

He put a finger over her lips. 'It would mean a good deal to me, Kezia. Honestly, I wouldn't ask you to if it wasn't important. You know that.' He looked at her with the smile she knew so well. 'What do you say?'

'I don't suppose it would hurt,' she said reluctantly.

'That's my girl!' He lifted her hand and touched it to his lips, and he smiled widely.

'You know, after you left this afternoon it did occur to me that you might come to blows with him, on account of his name and all.' Shann let go of her hand.

'His name?' Kezia frowned. 'What's wrong with

Devereaux? It's not a common name, but I'd scarcely hold an uncommon name against him.' She laughed, and then her laughter faded as her thoughts took her by surprise. Hold his name against him, no. But her salty damp sunkissed body, now that was a totally different thing. Good grief, she was allowing all this to get out of hand.

'You mean he didn't——' Shann stopped. 'I thought he said you'd met earlier in the day?'

'We did. At the office. But we weren't exactly formally introduced.' Kezia shrugged. 'He put his name down for one of the tours tomorrow. B. Devereaux.'

'I see. Just B. Devereaux.' Shann laughed. 'Maybe he had a premonition at that,' he chuckled away, enjoying himself.

'Shann, come on! What's the joke? What could be so amusing about a name beginning with B? Unless it's Bartholomew or,' she searched for an alternative, 'maybe Boris or Basil. Although I don't really think he looks like any of those.'

Shann shook his head. 'You'd never guess in a million years. But I'll give you a clue. Cast your mind back to the fateful voyage of the *Bounty* and our illustrious ancestors.'

Kezia frowned again. 'What's that got to do with it?'

Shann held up his hand to silence her. 'Who, Kezia McCoy, my fair descendant of those mutineers, did old Fletcher Christian heave into a longboat and send off to what he hoped would be good old Davy Jones' locker? None other than the dastardly Captain Bligh.'

'Captain Bligh?' she repeated.

'Oh, I don't think Devereaux would want to stand on ceremony. Just plain old Bligh would do nicely.'

Shann tapped Kezia's cheek with a finger. 'Knowing what a champion you are for the perpetuation of our heritage I thought you might have taken an exception to our friend's name.'

'Bligh Devereaux? Bligh?' she queried incredulously.

'I'm afraid so,' grinned Shann.

'But why would anyone want to call their son Bligh?' Kezia asked in amazement.

'Devereaux told me his father, who was a Navy man, held William Bligh in great esteem as a seaman and he also believed their family was distantly related to Bligh.' Shann gave a short laugh. 'That should go down well,' he added under his breath so that she wasn't quite sure he'd said exactly that. 'Anyway, let's go inside. Rae will be looking after Devereaux, but you're the one he's interested in, Kezia.'

'Shann, please, you're embarrassing me!'

He laughed as he climbed out of the car. 'Accept the compliment, Kez.' He held out his arm and slipped it about her waist as they entered the motel. 'The guy fancies you. So what? Isn't that every girl's dream? To have a guy fancy her?'

Kezia gave a breathless laugh. 'If you say so. And I guess he is only here on holiday. I mean, it's not as though he lives here on the island.'

'Well, no.' Shann's gaze slid away from her. 'Er, Kez ...' His eyes went back to her face and away again before his smile was back in place. 'Come on, let's go into dinner.'

They crossed the foyer and branched off to the left towards the restaurant.

'Did I tell you you look beautiful tonight?' Shann asked softly, his fingers tightening on her waist.

Kezia smiled shyly up at him. Shann thought she was beautiful. And at that moment she felt beautiful, because he had said she was and she had been dreaming about this particular moment for years and years.

Leaning closer, Shann kissed her fleetingly on the forehead, barely checking his stride. 'Devereaux has good taste,' he said as they entered the largish restaurant and crossed to join the couple already seated.

As her eyes met the vivid blueness of Devereaux's Kezia's smile faltered just a little. Somehow she knew those eyes had been on them from the moment she had entered the room with Shann, and as they walked up to the table Devereaux's piercing blue eyes went slowly downwards to the place where Shann's fingers rested lightly on Kazia's waist.

Immediately Shann removed his arm, ushering Kezia to the chair on Devereaux's right.

'Sorry, we're late. We were held up a little.' Shann sat down, smiling his charming smile at Raewyn.

Devereaux's eyes had narrowed, his lids shielding his expression, but Kezia could feel them as they went from Shann to herself, resting on the curve of her lips so that she had to call on all her willpower to still their tendency to tremble.

An olive-skinned young man in dark slacks and a brilliant white shirt materialised beside their table. 'Would you like to consult the menu now, sir?' he addressed Shann. 'Or perhaps you'd care for pre-dinner drinks?'

The young waiter was a friend of Chris's, and with her argument with her brother still fresh in her mind Kezia was more than aware of the surreptitious looks she was getting, as the waiter's dark eyes went interestedly from her to Shann to the dark-haired stranger, and she wondered wryly if Chris was going to hear about all that transpired at the table. A spurt of self-derisive amusement rose in her as it crossed her mind to wish she had the nerve to lean across and run her hand down the smooth material of the jacket straining over Devereaux's muscular forearm.

At that tantalising point her gaze met his and for one heart-stopping moment the flash of amusement lurking in his eyes made her suspect that he'd read her mind.

'Hey, Kez! Snap out of it!' Shann's voice, faintly touched with irritation, reached her.

'Oh! Sorry, Shann. Were you ... were you talking to me?' She flushed with embarrassment, and Rae's mocking look didn't help. It seemed to say she was making a naïve fool of herself as usual, so obviously mooning over their guest.

Shann's eyes settled on her flushed face and then flicked over to Bligh Devereaux, that same slight touch of irritation in the line of his mouth before he smiled and swept it away. 'I just asked if you'd like a drink before dinner. How about a Moselle? You like that, don't you?'

'That would be fine,' she replied, her hands clutched tightly together in her lap, wishing the floor would open up and swallow her. She'd have to learn to mask her feelings, stop letting them wash over her face.

Shann ordered the drinks and then the waiter handed them the elaborate menus. With a strong grip on herself Kezia exerted all her willpower to hold the menu with barely a tremor in her fingers.

'What can you recommend?' a deep voice asked beside her, and his dark head leaned closer to share her menu, his own lying untouched on the white lace tablecloth.

Her willpower broke up and set her back where she'd been a moment earlier. 'I can't really say. Shann's the one to ask for recommendations. I haven't——' she took a quick nervous breath, 'I don't dine out very much.'

'This sounds interesting.' His long finger tapped the sheet at the ornately written Red Emperor à la Cascade. 'I'm told the local fish is delicious.'

'Yes, it is.' So much for Chris's assertions that she would be able to talk under water!

'Did your brothers catch any, by the way?' he asked, still far too close to Kezia for her comfort.

'Yes, they did quite well,' she replied, wishing he would move back to his own side of the table.

'Chris and Toby been fishing?' Shann broke in.

Kezia nodded. 'This morning.' Had it only been this morning that she'd met this disturbing stranger?

'I must try to get away one morning. Chris has promised me a trip out in his new boat,' said Shann, glancing up as the waiter returned with their wine, pouring a little into a glass for Shann with a flourish. Shann raised the glass to his lips and then nodded his approval for the rest of the glasses to be poured.

'Kez? Rae? Decided what you want yet?' he asked them.

'Steak Diane for me,' Rae spoke for the first time, her voice just slightly bored.

'I'll have the fish,' Kezia told him quietly, relieved that Bligh Devereaux had straightened away from her.

'Same as Kezia for me,' he said firmly, and yet his

tone intimate, and his words shivered up her backbone prickling her skin.

What they talked about during that meal Kezia couldn't afterwards recall. She knew she ate the deliciously prepared local fish, that she drank a glass or two of wine and that she even chose a dessert, not being able to resist the brandy snaps. Apart from that she was vaguely aware of speaking when she was spoken to and that she even volunteered an occasional comment into the conversation. But afterwards she realised she might not have been there, her equilibrium was emotionally out of balance, and she was totally physically disorientated.

By the time the band struck up the first dance number Kezia was sure she was actually dreaming, that she'd wake up in her bed with the moonlight insinuating itself between the open blinds on her window.

However, as a strong hand settled over her own hand where it rested on the table she came right back to earth with a mind-clearing jolt.

'Would you excuse us?' he was saying to Shann and Rae, and then she was on the dance floor and in his arms.

He didn't attempt to hold her close to him, simply held her conventionally, guiding her around the small floor with an expertise she hadn't for a second doubted he'd possess.

She followed his lead mechanically, only aware that one of her hands was lost in his and the other rested on his broad shoulder. If she moved that hand just a little her fingertips would touch the tanned column of his throat above the collars of his pale blue shirt and grey suit coat. She shivered, and his eyes looked down at her.

'What was that for?' he asked, bending forward so that she could hear him above the band.

'I think someone walked over my grave,' she replied, her eyes fixing themselves on the knot of his tie, giving the conservatively coloured pattern on it her undivided attention, and as the song came to an end she allowed herself to glance up at him. 'Thank you for the dance.'

'Thank you, Kezia,' he said just as formally, but he was smiling and when she would have returned to their table he caught her hand. 'Let's stay for the next bracket.'

The female member of the group smiled at Kezia as she took the microphone and her eyes went to Kezia's partner with undisguised interest. Kezia groaned inwardly. She used to go to school with the singer, Rachel Adams, and judging by the look in Rachel's eye Kezia was in for an interrogation when they next met in the street!

Bligh Devereaux gave Kezia a sardonic look as the fast tempo began to throb, with Rachel throwing herself into her song, and he stood away from her, moving with the music. Kezia joined him, slightly selfconscious until the beat reached her and she relaxed, letting herself get with the rhythm. Her eyes were drawn to him, admiring the subtleness of his long lithe body as he danced easily without trying to draw attention to himself.

Rachel was singing a bracket of the faster Olivia Newton-John songs, and suddenly the suggestive words of the song reached Kezia and her eyes met Bligh Devereaux's. One eyelid flicked downwards in a wink and colour flooded her face even as the corners of her mouth lifted in an automatic smile.

From the up-tempo bracket the band went straight into a slower ballad and Kezia found herself drawn close to Bligh Devereaux's hard body, his arms around her, the warm male odour of his musky aftershave lotion filling her, and quivers of excitement began in the pit of her stomach, rising to quicken her heartbeats until they drummed in her ears.

'What was that about getting physical?' His husky tone played on her nerve ends while his breath fanned the hair at her temple as he made reference to the lyrics of the last song.

Somehow Kezia's hands had slid around his waist beneath his jacket which he had unbuttoned during the faster dance and the smooth silkiness of his shirt over his firm body literally took her breath away. Everything and everyone else faded in significance as she gave herself up to the wonder of this entirely new sensation.

Her questing fingertips found the slight indentation of his backbone and she felt his quick intake of breath before his arms pulled her impossibly closer to the solidness of his broad chest, his flat stomach, and the arousing pressure of his taut thighs. Kezia felt as though she was drowning, sliding downwards beneath the enveloping folds of a warm blue ocean to a world that at this infinite moment promised so much more, more soaring heights of her senses, to a plane of purely physical excitement.

Physical. The word played over in her mind. Physical. That's all it was, a physical thing, and she ... Her hands went back to his waist, exerting a pressure meant to put a little distance between them, but his strong arms locked about her determined to do just the opposite.

Her eyes rose to meet his and she called valiantly on her seemingly paralysed vocal chords.

'Mr Devereaux——' she began, and drew a steadying breath.

'The name's Bligh, Kezia,' he said huskily.

'I don't think . . .'

'Bligh, Kezia. Say it.' His words flowed over her, a soft command, holding her in the web of his potent attraction.

'Please, Bligh. I'd like . . . I think we should go back to the others,' she finished in a rush.

'Why?' His breath fanned her earlobe and his lips brushed the sweep of her neck. 'I like small parties.'

Kezia trembled and he raised his head, his eyes bright with that same amusement mixed with the unmistakable intensity of arousal that wiped any of her resistance right away in one fell swoop.

'Shann and Raewyn will wonder where we are. Besides, we're not being very sociable,' she tried at last, forcing the thought that she didn't want him to agree with her to the farthest corner of her mind.

'They don't seem to mind. They're dancing, too. He inclined his head and when Kezia's gaze followed his direction she saw the other couple dancing, deep in conversation, a serious one at that, if their expressions were anything to go by.

Just then Raewyn looked across and her green eyes met Kezia's, and the coldness in them made Kezia's steps falter. Rae's eyes burned with open dislike before she turned back to Shann. She glanced up at Bligh Devereaux, wondering if he'd seen the other girl's hostile expression. But he was looking down at her somewhat thoughtfully, and then he came closer again.

'Relax, Kezia,' that deep voice said softly in her ear, 'and enjoy the music.'

Relax, he said. She could almost laugh at that. To be held in his arms, her body so close to his, was not the most relaxing of experiences. It was totally disturbing, made even more so because Kezia had never before had to cope with the responses her body made with little attention to the conscious directives from her mind. It was as though her mind and her body were separate entities, things apart, and there was a communication breakdown somewhere between. And if she didn't set about rectifying the problem she could foresee no end of trouble, she admonished herself.

She was so completely aware of him, from the top of her head to the tips of her sandal-clad feet, and the feeling was exciting and stimulating and yet alarming, like nothing she had experienced before. Something told her that this was a fire, one that could rage way out of control, and that she should make some attempt to douse the flames before there was any threat of danger, but . . .

The smoothness of the material in his jacket was cool against her cheek and the musky male odour of him was an intoxicant. Would one evening hurt? What could happen in the middle of a dance floor? He was a very good dancer and it had been ages since she had spent an evening this way, so where was the harm? Ships that pass in the night, she told herself, and knew her traitorous body had won that round hands down.

Eventually, of course, the band took a break and Kezia returned to their table with a rueful reluctance. The time had come to get herself back into perspective, build some small defence against this far too attractive mainlander. And as long as he kept his distance she could manage that quite well.

Their table was empty when they reached it and Bligh Devereaux held her chair for her, his hand brushing her shoulder as he moved to his own seat and her skin prickled responsively to his touch. So much for her defences, she thought with a sinking feeling inside her.

'Would you care for another drink?' he asked her easily as she glanced about for Shann and Raewyn.

'Er—yes, please. A lemon squash would be nice, thanks. Dancing has made me thirsty.' She smiled at him. 'I wonder where the others are?'

He shook his head absently. 'Probably getting a drink, which I shall do as well.' He stood up. 'I won't be long.'

Kezia stood up, too. 'I'll just go and comb my hair while you're getting the drinks.'

His eyes moved over her dark loose curls and he smiled as he nodded and strode towards the bar.

Wending her way through a couple of tables, Kezia went out into the hall and turned to the right towards the ladies' powder room, her footfalls almost soundless on the carpeted floor. The sound of voices made her pause and turn back towards the restaurant entrance. At first she couldn't see anyone, but a movement behind the shield of a planter of greenery caught her eye seconds before Raewyn Bourke's angry voice made her hold back her intention to let Shann's secretary know she was nearby.

'I tell you, Shann, I'm getting thoroughly brassed off at the way she moons over you.' Raewyn's words came quietly but clearly through the leafy foliage in the divider. Although she wasn't speaking loudly what she was saying was angrily distinct.

'Come on, honey. It's perfectly harmless,' Shann spoke softer than Raewyn, his tone placating.

'Harmless, my eye! She's getting too old for it to be harmless. I could take it when it was just an adolescent crush, but I mean what I say, Shann. I'm fed up with it!'

'It won't be for much longer, you know that. The big fish is nibbling on the line very nicely,' Shann spoke confidently.

'And how do you know that for sure? Believe me, Shann, he's nobody's fool and it wouldn't do for you to underestimate him, even if he is in a state of bedazzlement over your little heroine,' she added sarcastically.

Shann laughed softly. 'In that case you've no need to worry where I'm concerned, have you?'

'That remains to be seen. She still thinks you're the best thing that's happened since frozen apple pie.'

'Don't you think so, too?' Shann's teasing tone dropped to a caress.

'Perhaps,' came the reluctant-sounding reply, Rae's voice a tone softer. 'Don't do that, Shann. You know it gets to me.'

'That's precisely why I do it,' he laughed, and the silence lengthened while Kezia stood transfixed, her face white as a sheet, her legs totally incapable of moving a muscle.

'Oh, Shann Evans,' Rae murmured, 'you're an out-and-out bastard.'

'Mm. If you say so,' Shann's reply was muffled.

'And this still doesn't mean that I like the situation any more then I did before.'

'I know, honey, and I'm sorry.' Shann sighed. 'Bear

with it all. It won't be for any longer than I can help, I promise.'

'God, some men are unpredictable! I don't know what he sees in her, and it's obvious that he sees something, that's for sure. I mean, she's pretty enough, but she's as naïve as they come. She's got virgin written all over her.'

'Hey, that's enough, Rae!' Shann broke in.

'Well, she has, for heaven's sake. That's why I can't understand a man in his position even noticing her. I mean, he must have his pick of them all, and from my observations his type of guy is always looking for a bit of experience.' Raewyn's voice dropped huskily. 'Aren't I right, lover?'

'We haven't got time to discuss that now,' Shann chuckled. 'But I think we might toss that point of view around later tonight. Right now, I think we should go back inside. I don't want Kezia wondering where we are. And I don't think I should leave her to Devereaux's sole attentions. He'll frighten her to death.'

'There you go again, Shann, treating her like some sort of fragile little ornament!' Rae's voice was full of anger once more. 'From what I've seen of her with her brother she manages to rule the roost without any trouble.'

'Rae! I've known Kezia all her life, and it's not easy for me to foist a man of the world like Bligh Devereaux on her, not without levelling with her.'

'You're too soft, Shann,' cut in Raewyn.

'Kezia'd do anything for me, Rae,' he said quietly.

'Anything?' Rae lowered her voice suggestively.

'Hell, Rae, give me a break! Kezia's a nice kid.' Shann said exasperatedly. 'Come on, let's go inside.'

Kezia moved then, stepping quickly into the alcove entrance to the ladies' room. Once inside the confining little room she stood pale-faced, staring at herself in the mirror above the washbasins, seeing only her expressionless face, her drooping figure as her mind spun uselessly.

Shann and Raewyn. Shann and Raewyn. She kept repeating the two names over and over in her head. Shann and Rae.

What a blind, naïve fool she was not to have noticed it before this! The signs, now she recognised them for what they were, had been as plain as the nose on a face. Raewyn Bourke was all any man could want in a woman. And working constantly with her Shann couldn't have failed to notice her, be attracted to her. Raewyn was beautiful, well-groomed, sophisticated, experienced. Yes, experienced. All that you're not, Kezia McCoy, she jeered herself. And she hasn't got 'virgin' written all over her either. Kezia closed her eyes and leant on the vanity basin.

Did everyone see her that way? Naïve? Boringly pure and prudish? Because that was how Raewyn made it sound—almost as though she had a disease or something. It wasn't that she was any less liberated in her outlook, Kezia wanted to tell Raewyn, it was simply that she hadn't felt she'd wanted to share her body with any of the young men she knew. To Kezia sleeping together was a precious part of loving and being loved, and she hadn't felt like that about anyone. Even the love she had for Shann, in her happy daydreams about him, she'd never thought about making love to him. What she felt for Shann was— well . . . She struggled to get it right in her thoughts and she began to wonder just what it was she had felt

for him. She'd loved him, she knew that, but ...
Perhaps it *had* been just a childish immature crush?

She cringed with embarrassment as parts of Rae's
conversation flooded back to taunt her again. How
they must have laughed at her youthful adoration of
Shann, and she felt a physical pain at the picture she
conjured up of Shann's amused indulgence.

And now the joke had worn off and become a source
of anger for Raewyn, although Shann could still use
her feelings for him as a lever to get her to play along
with whatever scheme he had in mind that involved
impressing Bligh Devereaux. God, she was a fool!
Kezia would do anything for me, Shann had said. And
she would have. She squeezed her eyes closed and her
even white teeth bit into her lip.

How was she ever going to face them again? It
seemed to her that her innermost soul had been ripped
open and her secret thoughts laid bare for the world to
see. Raewyn was right: she had adored Shann. And all
the while he had stood back knowing it, smiling
indulgently and then laughing over it with the other
girl.

Tears welled in her eyes, but she angrily blinked
them back, not allowing them to fall. Straightening
her back, she lifted her chin and stared defiantly at
her now flushed cheeks. Well, they wouldn't get the
chance to laugh at her again, she'd make sure of that.
She would push the Shann Evans of her girlish
dreams out of sight, as though he had never been, and
let him see that she had grown up, was far more
mature now about these things, and not the sweet little
virgin they imagined her to be.

But how? How was she going to go about it? It
wasn't something you could introduce into a conversa-

tion. A laugh and then a lightly said, 'Oh dear, I hope
I didn't embarrass you, Shann, with my adolescent
crush, because I'm all grown up now and quite
frankly, as a man you leave me cold.' She sighed,
knowing she couldn't possibly say anything like that
even if it had been true.

Slowly she removed the colourful hibiscus flower
from her hair and taking her brush from her purse
began to pull it through her tossled curls. The brush
stopped in mid-stroke as a thought crossed her mind.
Her fingers gripped the cold formica top. Could she
carry it off? Her knees went weak at the very
suggestion of it.

Shann said himself that Bligh Devereaux fancied
her, and a quiver of excitement twisted in her tummy
as she admitted to herself that this might be so. But
playing with Bligh Devereaux could—no, would—be
playing with fire, a raging inferno, she knew, but after
all, he was only here for a number of days, maybe a
week or two at the most, and she didn't have to live in
his pocket.

Nobody enjoyed discovering that their feelings,
given with love and admiration, were a source of
amusement to others. Her pride had been dented and
with Devereaux's unknowing assistance she might be
able to save just a little face. Yes, she'd do it. At least
it would give Shann Evans something to think about.
And Raewyn Bourke, for that matter.

CHAPTER FOUR

THE three of them, Shann, Raewyn and Bligh
Devereaux, were sitting at their table when Kezia
returned to the restaurant, and as she walked behind
Devereaux's chair her hand slipped lightly and
fleetingly across the breadth of his shoulders. He stood
up immediately and held her chair for her, and the
smile she gave him as she looked up at him was as
intimate as her nervousness would allow. Her smile
must have worked, for his hands lingered momentarily
on the coolness of her upper arms before he returned
to his own seat. Lifting the glass of frosting lemon
squash that was on the table in front of her, she took a
sip, her voice husky as she thanked him, the skin of
her arms still tingling from his touch.

She very nearly lost her nerve then, but beneath her
lowered lashes she shot a quick measuring glance at
the other couple, surprising a shadow of a frown on
Shann's face as he watched them, and she knew a brief
surge of satisfaction that her little ploy appeared to be
working. You see, Shann Evans, she wanted to cry,
my blinkers are off and I can see you aren't the only
fish in the sea!

'Well,' Shann gave a hearty laugh, 'what did you
think of the band, you two? You seemed to be
enjoying it out there.'

Bligh Devereaux inclined his head and sipped his
own drink.

'They're quite good, aren't they?' Kezia kept her

63

voice even and matter-of-fact. 'Much improved since the last time I heard them just after they formed up.'

Shann nodded. 'Having Rachel join them a couple of months ago gave the group a lift, too. She hasn't got a bad voice and she can put herself over well. About your age, isn't she, Kezia?'

'Yes. About.' Kezia just stopped herself from admitting that Rachel Adams was a year or two older than she was. 'Her young brother is one of Toby's best mates,' she improvised quickly.

'They seem popular with everyone,' Shann continued, looking at Bligh Devereaux. 'I've had them on permanently for some time now.'

The band began to play again as Shann finished speaking and he gave another strained laugh. 'Right on cue! How about dancing with me, Kez? I can't miss the opportunity now that I've got you here.'

Out of the corner of her eye Kezia caught the flash of momentary astonishment in the look Raewyn cast in Shann's direction and she hesitated. If she was going to carry out her plan . . .

'With your permission to borrow your partner, of course,' Shann smiled across at Bligh Devereaux.

Barely waiting for any acquiescence from the other man, Shann took Kezia's hand and led her on to the dance floor, pulling her into his arms, holding her almost as close as Bligh Devereaux had done. And Kezia could only allow herself to be taken along, sensing a tightness that had been in the air between the two men, loathe to even surmise at its reason.

Although Shann was quite a good dancer he hadn't the sublety of movement that Bligh Devereaux possessed, and Kezia cast a quick glance up at Shann, wondering with a twinge of despair almost akin to guilt where the magic had gone. As late as yesterday she would have given almost anything to be this close to Shann Evans. And now it had all fallen flat. Just because of a little more attractive than average mainlander, she amended to herself.

'Mmm, love your perfume,' Shann murmured in her ear, bringing her back to reality with a start.

'Thank you,' she replied. 'It was a birthday present from Chris.'

'You know, we dance together as though we were made for each other,' Shann smiled down into her eyes. 'How come we haven't done it before this?'

'Maybe because you didn't ask me,' she replied softly, amazed that she hadn't noticed before how easily Shann could switch his own brand of charm on and off. And she had known him all her life, thought she knew him best of all.

There was a flicker in his eyes, as though he was momentarily searching her expression for a hidden meaning, before he laughed a little uneasily.

'And in reply I'm afraid all I can say is that I must have been blind. We'll have to remedy my oversight, make up for lost time.'

When Kezia didn't reply Shann pulled her a little closer and they danced on in silence for a while until he spoke again.

'By the way, thanks for playing up to Devereaux for me. You're a real doll, Kez.' He glanced down at her, his smile all confidence. 'You're doing marvellously. If I hadn't known better you would have had me convinced that out on the dance floor you were enjoying cuddling up to him like a kitten.'

She laughed then, if somewhat breathlessly. 'I'd hardly call it cuddling up, Shann,' she said, pushing aside the flash of awareness at the remembered feel of Bligh Devereaux's hard body moving with hers.

'It looked very smoochy from where I stood,' remarked Shann dryly.

'We were just dancing close together,' Kezia looked up at him through her lashes, 'like we are now.'

'Not quite like we are. You'd have been hard pressed getting a cigarette paper between you and Devereaux.' Shann's voice had lost some of its teasing humour.

Kezia shrugged, not quite knowing what to say.

'You know, when I said give him some attention I didn't mean to throw your hat over the windmill for him.' A small irritated frown creased his forehead.

'Shann!' she laughed softly, realising she was enjoying this moment of feminine power. Shann was reacting as though he was jealous, although why he should be she couldn't imagine. He had never really sought her out or treated her as anything other than Chris's young sister. So why go all possessive now? Unless he was playing dog-in-the-manger, not interested in her until someone else showed signs of being so. Whichever way she looked at it Shann was being childish. Surely Raewyn was more than enough woman for him!

And with that thought came a spurt of anger. What right had Shann to get uptight about her attention to Bligh Devereaux? Only minutes ago he had been kissing Raewyn Bourke. 'Look, Shann,' her smile faded, 'I only met the man today and, apart from that, I don't think you have any right to come on all heavy. I'm old enough to please myself, surely?'

'He's no easygoing island guy, Kezia.' Shann was really frowning now. 'He's been through the mill more than once and I'll bet he didn't lack for females falling all over themselves to be asked along for the ride. Take it from me, Kezia, Devereaux's got experience written all over him.'

'He has?' Finding the situation suddenly funny, Kezia forced down a giggle, half nervous amusement, half a sense of teasing anticipation. 'What kind of experience do you mean specifically, Shann?'

'Hell, Kezia, I'm serious!' Shann looked put out. 'The guy's a very well known, very powerful businessman and he knows where it's all at, you take it from me. Little girls like you, all starry-eyed and innocent, would be a pushover for him if he turned on his charm.'

'You're only making me more interested, Shann,' Kezia laughed up at him. 'Maybe it's time I picked up a bit of experience myself, and if he's the expert you say he is, well——' she left the sentence hanging between them.

'Cut that out, Kezia,' Shann snapped at her. 'It doesn't suit you.'

'You're beginning to sound like Chris, and that I don't need,' Kezia bit back. 'I'm a big girl now, and it may surprise you to know, Shann Evans, that I do know how to handle men like Devereaux.' She looked determindly up at Shann and ignored the tiny voice somewhere inside her that jeered at her, demanding to know exactly who she thought she was kidding.

'For heaven's sake, Kezia, I don't want to argue with you.' Shann's voice dropped lower. 'I care about you, and therefore I worry about you.'

First Chris and now Shann, both intent on wrapping her in cottonwool. Kezia sighed. 'There's no need to, Shann.'

'Well, I do. I've known you a long time and,' he bent his head and kissed her cheek, 'what's more, I think you're one of the nicest girls I know.'

'Thanks,' she said, pulling a face at him.

'And the most attractive,' Shann laughed, his eyes running over her upturned face. 'Very attractive indeed.' His expression changed, becoming more serious now.

'As attractive as Raewyn?' The words came out before she could stop them.

Shann started in surprise and then his eyes slid away from hers.

'Hey, Kezia! Raewyn and I are just friends,' he laughed. 'Workmates.'

'And I'm just friends with Bligh Devereaux.' She forced herself to smile back at him, leaving Shann with nothing more to say, although he watched her pointedly with a suggestion of a frown for the remainder of the evening.

A hand on her shoulder dragged Kezia reluctantly from sleep next morning and she rolled over to blink up at her mother, who was standing by her bed. It seemed like only moments since she had eventually dozed off.

After Shann had driven her home, not allowing Bligh Devereaux the chance to offer to drive her himself, she had been far too mentally stimulated to even contemplate sleep. There had been a slight atmosphere between Shann and herself since their conversation on the dance floor and she had been pleased to reach the haven of her room.

But sleep hadn't come, of course. The evening had given her much too much to think about, to mull over, and if she was honest with herself she would have to admit the Kezia McCoy of that evening was not the Kezia McCoy she knew so well. The new Kezia McCoy was a flirt, an amateur one, admittedly, but a flirt for all that, and Kezia had a feeling she wasn't going to like herself in the cold light of day.

'Mum? What time is it? Have I slept in?' she asked sleepily. But surely it was her day off?

'Sorry to wake you, love, but Meg's just phoned me,' frowned Allie McCoy. 'She's sprained her ankle rather badly and can't take the tour today. I hate asking you, Kez, on your day off especially, but there's no one else. How about doing it for me?'

'Oh, Mum!' Kezia sighed tiredly, wishing she could return to the peaceful oblivion of non-thinking sleep. 'What about Sue?'

'She's doing the half-day tour,' replied her mother. 'I tried to get her to do the full day and give you the half-day, but she's taking the kids to the dentist this afternoon. Sorry, Kez.'

'That's okay, Mum. I guess it can't be helped.' Kezia sat up resignedly. 'How long have I got to get ready?'

Her mother patted her arm and smiled down at her. 'Long enough to have breakfast. I've cooked you bacon and eggs.'

'Bribery, Mum?' she smiled back.

'No. Thanks in anticipation,' Allie laughed as she left the room.

Luckily Kezia had a fresh uniform ironed, and it was only as she pulled the bright orange shirt waister dress over her head and smoothed the white contrasting collar that she remembered that Bligh Devereaux was booked on the full day tour, and her heart skipped erratically for a few moments before it sank with a guilty dread. A whole day in his company.

Oh dear, to have to face him so soon! She hoped he hadn't got the wrong idea last night. What with one thing and another she had been rather attentive. Very attentive. She grimaced. How could he help getting the wrong idea? she asked herself as she picked up her brush and pulled it vigorously through her hair.

Damn Shann Evans! It was all his fault. Her brush halted in mid-stroke. No, it wasn't really. She'd brought it all on herself because her foolish pride had been wounded. A little ache over her heart twinged for the dream bubble of love she'd had for Shann that had been burst last night and a lump rose in her throat.

Her eyes moved over the face that stared back at her from her mirror. There's no point in crying, she chastised herself. Besides, Shann wasn't worth it. She lifted her chin and dared herself to let the threatening tears overflow. And self-pity wouldn't help either, she told herself, putting her brush back on her dressing table. Regardless of whose fault last night was, she knew she was going to have to ever so gently and firmly extricate herself from Bligh Devereaux.

'You won't have to fill the bus with petrol,' her mother smiled at her as she put a plate of crisp bacon and a golden egg in front of Kezia. 'I told Chris to do that for you before he left. He's taken a party of Americans out fishing for the day, and Toby's gone with them.'

'I'll check it anyway,' Kezia pulled a face. 'Not that I don't trust Chris, but I don't trust him, knowing him of old.'

'Perhaps he needs to have a little more responsibility,' said her mother quietly. 'Maybe we mollycoddle him too much.'

'He's twenty-three, Mum. He's hardly a child. He should be able to take responsibility without having it given to him.' Kezia frowned. 'I was absolutely livid with him over those services on the cars yesterday morning. He promised to do them.'

'I know. I was mad with him, too. I gave him the rounds of the kitchen last night when I came home,' Allie assured her.

'Mm. In one ear and out the other,' Kezia muttered, and yawned.

'Kezia, are you sure you don't mind taking the tour today? You look a bit peaky.' Her mother regarded her worriedly. 'Would you prefer to do my office work and I'll take the bus?'

'No, I don't mind, Mum. I'd rather be out and about than cooped up inside.'

Allie McCoy looked steadily at her daughter. 'You haven't had a holiday in ages, love. Tell you what, when Toby goes back to Brisbane to school why don't you go with him? I know your aunt wouldn't mind having you to stay for a couple of weeks, and you could have a nice rest. You can't get that around here.'

'You seem to forget you haven't had a holiday yourself, Mum,' Kezia reminded her mother.

'Oh, me! I've got the least strenuous bit to do.' Allie waved her hand airily. 'All I do is write down the bookings and answer the phone.'

Kezia sighed again, gazing absently at the piece of toast she was eating. Perhaps she should get away for a short while, give herself time to get herself sorted out.

'Think it over anyway, love,' her mother was saying. 'It's still two weeks before Toby goes back to school.'

'All right. Well, I'd best be off. See you later, Mum.' She stood up and took the keys to the small bus off the hook and held them up for her mother to see. 'So much for Chris filling the bus tank with petrol,' she said dryly as she walked out to her motorcycle.

With the small tourist bus backed out of the garage and fuelled up Kezia arranged a row of colourful hibiscus blooms and leaf greenery along the top of the dashboard before walking through to the office and collecting her list of bookings for the tour. She quickly tallied up the numbers and the various hotels and motels she would have to visit to collect her party of tourists. There was only one booking from Cascade Court and she knew she could pick up Bligh Devereaux first, or last. Flicking the ignition, she sat with the motor idling for a few moments, her fingers tapping uncharacteristically on the steering wheel before she cast aside a twinge of cowardice, set the bus in gear and turned in the opposite direction to Cascade Court and the waiting Bligh Devereaux.

Most of the twenty or so people she collected were middle-aged, with only two young couples in their twenties, and they were either Australians or New Zealanders. They seemed a pleasant, easygoing group, although Kezia was a little wary of one middle-aged matron with a thin dissatisfied mouth who was touring with her sister.

Eventually there was only Cascade Court left, and a tiny pulse began to flutter in her throat as she turned the bus into the driveway and pulled to a halt at the entrance to the motel.

Bligh Devereaux didn't appear to be waiting within sight of the entrance, so Kezia climbed out of the bus and strode up the steps into the foyer. Shann was at the reception desk and he replaced the phone on its cradle as she approached.

'Morning, Kez.' He smiled broadly, his charm in evidence once again. He was apparently over his fit of the sulks.

'Hello, Shann,' Kezia replied evenly. 'Could you ring Bligh Devereaux's room and tell him I'm here. For the tour,' she added quickly as Shann raised his eyebrows.

'Okay.' He reached for the phone again. 'I thought it was your day off. Or did you change so that you could spend the day with him?' he asked, his voice teasing, although there was an underlying note of testiness.

'Meg sprained her ankle,' she told him, not rising to his bait, 'so I had to take over.'

'Poor old Kez!' He leant forward, his elbows resting on the desk. 'How about coming out to dinner with me when I can get away? Just the two of us. I've been meaning to ask you for ages.'

'Well, I . . .' Kezia swallowed, her face flushing. She would have jumped at the chance of an evening out with Shann if it hadn't been for overhearing Raewyn last night.

'You know, you look gorgeous when you blush,' he said softly, his tone lowly intimate, his hand moving to cup her cheek. 'Absolutely gorgeous,' he repeated almost to himself.

'Shann, please, I don't think——' Kezia stopped as Shann's gaze slid past her and she spun around, knowing who she'd see behind her.

The thick pile carpet had deadened his footfalls and he stopped beside Kezia to lean lithely on the desk.

'Hello, Kezia.'

His voice was every bit as deep as she remembered

it from the evening before, and it played even greater havoc with her senses. Her whole body was warmed by the heat of his potent attraction. He wore light cream slacks and a dark brown knit shirt with two contrasting cream stripes across the breadth of his chest and around the short sleeves. With his hair still damp from his shower he was so vital and fit-looking that Kezia's eyes refused to be drawn away from him.

'I've come to collect you for the tour,' she got out if somewhat unevenly, as she dragged her wayward thoughts into a little order. So much for extricating herself from him. One look at him and she'd all but fallen at his feet, she thought wryly.

'Well, here I am. And I'm looking forward to it, too,' he smiled, and her legs wobbled alarmingly.

He really was nice looking, she admitted to herself, as her eyes flicked back to his. She saw his keen gaze take in Shann's lounging figure, his hand now resting on Kezia's arm as she in turn leant on the desk and then his vivid blue eyes held hers, a faint guardedness in their lash-shielded depths.

'That's good,' Kezia swallowed, trying to pull herself together. 'I'm sure you're going to enjoy it. Shall we go?' She glanced back at Shann. ' 'Bye, Shann.'

'Kezia?' Shann's hand on her arm tightened as she went to pull away from him. 'About that other matter we were discussing . . .'

'I'll . . . I have to go now, Shann,' she said quickly, not committing herself. 'We've a full day ahead of us.'

He let her go, a frown on his brow giving him that same almost sulky look, and she hurried across to the entrance, catching up with Bligh Devereaux as he reached the bus. He took a vacant seat halfway up the aisle and if she raised her eyes to the rear vision mirror his blue eyes were watching her.

Pulling her gaze from his, she forced herself to concentrate on the passengers en masse. It was her job to give them an interesting and informative tour of the island, and it was something she always enjoyed doing. Today would be no exception. She would just have to put her awareness of that particular mainlander to the very back of her mind and concentrate on the job in hand.

As she deftly engaged a low gear heading down the steep Taylor's Road she welcomed her group firstly in English and then in the soft lilting dialect of the Norfolk Islanders, a mixture of eighteenth-century English, Weslh, Irish and Tahitian.

They officially began the tour at Kingston, but she pointed out various landmarks along their way, explaining that Watermill Valley through which they were passing, with its ruined watermill and restored dam, was one of the oldest settlements on Norfolk. Now only cattle grazed where once hard-driven convicts tilled the soil. The one hundred Norfolk pines lining the roadside were planted to com- memorate Aunt Jemima Robinson, a well-known Norfolk Islander who had died just after reaching her hundredth birthday.

Pulling the bus to a halt on a stretch of grassy lawn that commanded a view of the Kingston ruins, Kezia began to point out various sections of the settlement. Everyone sat quietly as she spoke into the microphone. Kezia had a fierce pride in her heritage and it showed in her rendition of the story of the Norfolk Islanders.

Norfolk Island itself, she told them in her soft attractive voice, had been discovered in 1774 by

Captain James Cook during his second voyage
around the world and the first of the two penal
settlements was begun in 1788. The second settlement established in 1825 was an extremely harsh
one, with only the very worst convicts sent from
New South Wales and Van Diemen's Land. And it
was for this penal harshness that Norfolk Island had
become notorious.

However, the cost of upkeep on the colony became
too great and the island was suggested as a home for
the Pitcairn Islanders, who had outgrown their own
island. The Pitcairners were nearly all descendants of
the mutineets from the *Bounty* and a number of
Tahitian women, and in 1856 a party numbering over
one hundred and ninety landed in Norfolk Island.
They bore such names as Adams, Christian, Evans,
Quintel, McCoy, Buffet, Nobbs and Young.

Kezia never tired of telling her story, making the
ruins come to life. The gruesome Gallow's Gate which
had sometimes been a welcome release from a harsh
and wretched life. The stark symmetry of the Military
Barracks building erected in 1836. The imposing
Government House, where the Commandants resided
and sentries used to pace, overlooking green fields
once cultivated by bitter, resentful men driven by
relentless overseers. The neatly restored picture-
squeness of the residences along Quality Row. And
the arrival, after five weeks of wearying seasickness, of
the Pitcairners, landing in a strange bewildering place
amid squalls of drenching rain.

A number of people asked questions which Kezia
answered as she drove along the sea-front past the
lime kiln, around to the far side of Emily Bay where a
couple of photography buffs climbed out of the bus to

take photos along the bay towards the ruins. The sun glistened on the turquoise water.

'What a nice calm little bay,' remarked an elderly lady. 'Is it safe for swimming?'

Unconsciously Kezia's eyes met Bligh Devereaux's in the rear view mirror, and she felt herself blush as she assured the lady that it was most certainly safe for swimming. For swimming, yes, piped up an inner voice, but not quite so safe for sharing the raft with handsome, so-sure-of-themselves mainlanders. And her heart was still tripping over itself as she drove on along past the cemetery, recommending a walk through the older section where headstones dated back to the early 1800s. At Bloody Bridge, the largest bridge on the island, she related the grisly tale of a harsh overseer who was supposedly murdered by a group of convicts constructing the bridge. The body was said to have been walled up in the bridge, but telltale blood seeped through, leading to the discovery of the murder and the execution of the culprits.

At Queen Elizabeth Lookout on Rooty Hill Road everyone climbed out to view the ruins of Kingston from the high vantage point. Morning tea of fresh fruit, bananas and oranges was taken overlooking the indigo blue of Ball Bay and the Pacific Ocean, and all at once it was lunchtime and Kezia turned the bus through the gates of Bishop's Court, a neat old island homestead, where the tourists were provided with a smörgasborg meal.

Kezia moved about helping organise the food, seeing everyone served themselves until they were all seated at the bench tables set out on the wide verandah overlooking the neatly kept lawns. Only then did she spoon servings of the cold meat cuts and salads on to a plate for herself.

Intending to sit with a group of four elderly ladies who were holidaying together from Tasmania, she walked around the first two tables, only to be halted by a hand on her arm as she passed the third table.

'I've saved you a seat.' Bligh Devereaux's voice sent shockwaves of tingling sensations down her spine.

As she paused, held by the grip of his strong fingers on her cool skin and his even more forceful magnetism, he exerted a minimum of pressure and she found herself seated beside him, his hard thigh resting against her leg. Kezia's stomach began to quiver and she swallowed nervously.

This was no good at all. She was behaving like a Victorian maiden! She made a determined effort to turn to him with her usual easy naturalness.

'Well, how are you enjoying the tour so far?' she asked him, keeping her voice as steady and friendly as she could manage, using the fact that she was settling herself at the table as an excuse to move away from the disturbance actually touching him was creating inside her.

'I'm enjoying it very much,' he replied, smiling at her, his eyes moving over her, unseating her carefully mustered calm. 'I can't believe the beauty of the island,' he added. 'And I don't just mean the scenery. I'm talking about the island as a whole—the people, their friendliness, their attitude to life.'

Kezia smiled back at him, pleased with his obvious sincerity.

'We must guard against losing it,' he said softly almost to himself as he turned back to his meal. 'It's a lost quality these days, this open friendliness,' he added.

Kezia warmed to him. She never tired of hearing tourists compliment the home she loved, and she relaxed, enjoying sitting beside him as they ate the deliciously prepared food.

'Are you really related to Captain Bligh?' she asked him in her new-found companionship.

He raised his eyebrows in surprise.

'Shann Evans mentioned it to me,' she explained. 'I hope you don't mind. 'I——' she paused, 'I . . . Bligh isn't a common name, especially used as a Christian name.' She flushed, remembering Shann's derogatory teasing when he spoke about Devereaux and his unusual name.

'My father believes we're directly descended from one of Bligh's daughters. He had six or so, I believe.' He smiled at her. 'That we're actually related to Bligh is just word of mouth handed down through the family, but my father is working on proving the story at the moment. It gives him an interest now he's retired. He's also made a study of Bligh's career and has always admired him.' He shrugged. 'Hence my name, for good or bad.'

'But weren't you teased about it as a child?' she asked him.

'I guess so.' He laughed. 'But as you can see, I overcame such an overwhelming disadvantage.'

The same tingling sensation stirred inside Kezia as his blue eyes crinkled up as he laughed, the corners of his mouth lifting, driving attractive lines down his cheeks, his strong teeth white against his mahogany tan.

'Goodness!' She broke his gaze to glance at her watch. 'I'd better see to the tea and coffee.' She stood up, knowing a flash of reluctance to interrupt their conversation, but when she made to move across to the small table containing a large urn he followed her and began sorting out the cups and saucers.

Kezia knew she should object to his helping. He was, after all, a tour guest, but he smiled crookedly at her and all she could do was smile back, watching as he dealt with the mêlée as everyone came forward to collect their respective cups, his smile charming one table of ladies to unrestrained laughter.

That smile should be registered as a dangerous weapon, Kezia thought as she smiled to herself. Like the rest of Bligh Devereaux. She watched him bend solicitously over the middle-aged lady with the prim dissatisfied mouth, seeing that mouth relax into a not-often-used smile. Far too charming for his own good, she told herself firmly. For his own good and hers, she decided ruefully.

Her mother was surely right. He was certainly attractive. If he hadn't been a mainlander . . . She overfilled a coffee cup and took herself sternly to task. She was mooning about like a schoolgirl with a king-size crush!

Her thoughts echoed Raewyn's words of the night before and a pain twisted inside her, bringing all the humiliation and embarrassment vividly back to her. Well, she wasn't going to make that same mistake twice, and she forced all fanciful thoughts about Bligh Devereaux from her mind. She wasn't ready to take any chances with him, she was sure of that.

Straight after lunch they walked across the road to the mission church, St Barnabas' Chapel, built of local stone and dedicated in 1880, admiring the marble floor, the rose window and the other stained glass panels in the apse.

Kezia drove the familiar route past Anson Bay where the strong wind buffeted the bus, to Point Howe overlooking Duncombe Bay where Captain Cook had first landed on the uninhabited island. She told her group that these cliffs were a breeding ground for muttonbirds, who burrow into the ground, their eerie mournful moaning cries earning them the local name 'ghost birds'.

As the full day tour drew to an end Kezia turned the bus along her favourite part of the entire trip, up the narrow winding Mount Pitt Road to the summit of the mountain. In parts those on the right-hand side of the bus gasped as the valley fell sharply away, the hillside a tangle of ferns, palms and vines.

In the small clearing at the top everyone climbed out of the bus for the breathtaking view of the whole island. Kezia pointed out the islands, the smaller flatter Nepean and the volcanic contours of Philip, the ruins of Kingston, the airstrip, the thick forest over Duncombe Bay, and she took a deep breath, feeling the exhilaration she always experienced at the top of her world.

Scattered houses nestled in between the dark green majestic pines and winding roads snaked lightly through the spread of greens. She sighed appreciatively, and then felt Devereaux's eyes on her, watching her, reaching down into her very soul, and she felt somehow naked and vulnerable, and she looked away, fearful, knowing she would have to guard herself against him, for those vivid blue eyes saw far too much.

CHAPTER FIVE

'KEZIA.' His voice on the phone was low and husky and she sat down rather suddenly as the shock of hearing his voice washed over her in waves.

The afternoon had seemed to end all too quickly after those few moments on Mount Pitt when he had seemed so close to her, close in spirit, so much closer than a simple physical nearness. They had met soul to soul in those immeasurable seconds, and Kezia knew that emotionally she had turned and run, unable to face the attraction they both knew burned between them. But she had been afraid, frightened by the implications, of an unknown world, a dark uncharted sea, unsure of herself and her ability to keep her control.

'Have dinner with me tonight?' Bligh asked softly, setting her blood pounding through her body like molten fire.

To accept his invitation, to be alone with him would be the very height of folly, rather like walking into a lion's lair just on feeding time. She'd be a fool to even contemplate such a thing. He was a holidaymaker, a tourist out for a good time, just as Chris said he was.

'Dinner?' Her voice sounded faraway, unlike her own. 'Thank you, I'd like that very much,' in disbelief she heard herself say.

'Fine.' She knew he was smiling and her stomach turned right over. 'I believe Barney Duffy's is worth a visit?'

'Yes, it is very nice. My favourite, in fact,' she added breathlessly, to the sound of her heartbeats pounding in her ears like the not so distant ocean.

'Good. Then Barney Duffy's it is,' he said. 'Shann Evans recommended it to me.'

'Oh.' Kezia stared at her fingers as they nervously twisted the fringe on the embroidered cloth on the telephone stand, wondering if she had only imagined the slight change in the timbre of his voice as he mentioned the other man.

'Would seven suit you?' he broke the silence that had fallen between them.

'Yes, seven would be fine. Shall I . . .' Kezia swallowed. 'Shall I call for you?'

He laughed softly then. 'No, I'll do the calling. I have the loan of a car and directions to your house, so I'll see you at seven.'

Kezia replaced the receiver, trying to quell the surge of anticipatory excitement that was growing to mammoth proportions inside her.

'Who was that? Shann Evans?' Her mother's voice brought her back to earth with a thud. Allie McCoy was smiling at the glow of colour that stained her daughter's face.

'No.' Kezia replied reluctantly, feeling her blush deepen and she unconsciously smoothed the folds of her skirt. 'Acutally, it was Mr Devereaux—Bligh Devereaux.'

'Oh,' smiled her mother knowingly, and walked away.

Barney Duffy's Restaurant was a rectangular box of a place sitting on its own just outside the Burnt Pine Shopping Centre. It was a popular haunt and the meals were superb.

The name Barney Duffy was taken from the legend of an escaped prisoner. In the early days the island had been more heavily wooded, the bush denser, providing concealment of sorts for absconders, one such being Barney Duffy, who had supposedly avoided recapture for over seven years, making his home and hiding place in a hollow pine tree. Kezia watched Bligh Devereaux from beneath her lashes as they sat at the small table in the restaurant and he read Barney Duffy's story on the colourful place-mats.

The legend went that two young soldiers returning from a fishing trip to Headstone came upon Barney Duffy and took him back to King's Town. Barney Duffy then made his horrible curse, vowing that his captors would die violent deaths before he had been dead a week. Of course Barney Duffy was tried and hanged at the Gallows Gate, and two days later the bodies of the two young soldiers were found floating in the sea off Headstone.

'It makes for an interesting story, doesn't it?' Bligh smiled at her.

'I always thought it was sad that he was caught after eluding everyone for so long,' she said wistfully her mind picturing the island in the late 1700s and the plight of a desperate man.

'You would have let him be?' He raised a slightly cynical eyebrow.

'I'm afraid so,' she replied. 'He wasn't harming anyone.'

'But he *was* a convict.'

'Yes, and most probably only because he stole a loaf of bread to feed his family.' Kezia's eyes sparkled. 'Or dared to have different political leanings from someone else with a bit of clout.'

Bligh held up his hand and grinned wryly at her. 'Hold it, Kezia. I see that light in your eyes and I don't want any disputes to ruin our evening. Okay? Peace for tonight?'

She smiled slowly and nodded. 'Peace. Maybe we should find a less provoking topic of conversation.'

He raised his eyebrows again. 'Something tells me that even a topic as mundane as the weather could get very stormy around us!'

His eyes moved over her face and the air space between them seemed to glow with their mutual awareness. Mesmerised by the almost blue-black coals of his eyes, Kezia's gaze locked with his and her breath caught painfully in her throat. When she thought she could bear it no longer his square jaw relaxed a little and he picked up the menu.

'Food,' he said, almost to himself. 'What do you recommend, Kezia?' he asked evenly enough, although his eyes continued to watch her.

They both decided on grilled steak and fresh garden side salad, and by the time they had finished that and the wine Bligh chose they were back on their easy footing, those tension-filled moments behind them, on the surface at least. Just how deeply buried those moments were Kezia didn't want to put to the test, knowing exactly how vulnerable she was when it came to this handsome confident stranger.

As she spooned a purple-black boysenberry from her parfait dessert into her mouth she realised that although she had been talking easily to him about herself and her family Bligh Devereaux hadn't spoken at all of his own background in Queensland. In fact, she knew no more about him now than she had before they began their evening.

'What do you do for a living?' she smiled at him, the question coming easily as he sat back enjoying a cigarette with his coffee. 'I mean, Shann said you were a businessman.'

'That's about it,' he replied, and his eyes left her face to settle on the empty wine glass he began twisting between his fingers.

'And are you successful?' Kezia's voice was mildly teasing, enjoying their easy intimacy.

He shrugged slightly, setting the wine glass back on the table. 'I suppose you could say I've had some measure of success,' he said wryly.

Kezia laughed softly. 'I was only teasing you. I knew you were successful.' Her eyes moved over him quickly, the pale blue tailored safari suit and contrasting dark blue shirt, the way he held himself, his overall aura of prosperity. 'You look successful,' she finished a little breathlessly.

'Thank you.' He inclined his dark head.

'What sort of business do you have?' she persisted, her smile faltering a little as that same guardedness clouded his expression.

'I have a couple of properties, a restaurant in Brisbane, that sort of thing,' he replied carefully after a short pause.

'Oh.' Kezia watched him surreptitiously and wondered if perhaps he was lying. But why would he lie? There was no reason for him to do so. Unless his business interests were on the shady side.

She shot a quick glance at him through her lashes. No, he definitely didn't look like that type of person. Kezia smiled derisively to herself. How would she know what that type of person looked like anyway? And besides, if he was a gangster type he would hardly be likely to admit it, that was for sure.

She went to ask him about his family and then stopped herself, flushing as it suddenly occurred to her that he might think she was prying. Her eyes slid to the bare third finger on his left hand and she wondered again if he was married. The idea that he was bound physically and emotionally to an unknown woman made her heart lurch painfully in her breast for some inexplicable reason. She took a hurried sip of her wine and set the glass unsteadily back on the table, her flow of conversation drying up completely.

Bligh himself also seemed lost in his own thoughts, his face expressionless, although his mouth seemed tense and a shadow of a frown brushed his forehead. His attention seemed to be held motionless on his empty wine glass.

'What made you decide to visit Norfolk Island?' Kezia asked him at last, disturbed by the constrained silence, not understanding the flow of undercurrents, thinking the question was innocent enough, uncomplicated and uncompromising.

He raised his eyes to her then and they regarded her broodingly before he smiled. 'The tourist brochures promised a peaceful, restful paradise,' he told her. 'It sounded ideal, so——' he shrugged.

'I suppose I'm prejudiced, but it is a paradise to me,' she said quietly. 'I wouldn't want to live anywhere else.'

'And have you seen any more of the world, young Kezia?' he laughed softly, his good humour returning, making him appear younger.

'I've been to the mainland, to Sydney and Brisbane. And once I went down to New Zealand,' she replied somewhat defensively. 'The people away aren't as friendly as they are here at home.'

He sipped his coffee. 'You've got a point there. We're all in too much of a hurry to stop, far to defensive to be friendly to strangers, always ready to take someone down before he takes you.' He frowned down at the tip of his cigarette. 'You have a treasure here worth more than worldly possessions,' he said softly and sincerely.

Kezia gazed back at him, her heart contracting. 'Thank you. I hope we can preserve it for ever.'

'I hope so, too.' He glanced at his wristwatch. 'Are you working tomorrow?' he asked, and she nodded. 'Then I guess I should get you home. It's ten-thirty already. Like another coffee before we go?'

Kezia shook her head, not trusting her voice, wishing she had the nerve to tell him she'd drink a dozen cups of coffee if it would prolong their evening. Bligh Devereaux was so different from anyone else she knew. She'd been out before quite often with young friends, but none of them were even remotely as exciting, as stimulating, as terrifying as Bligh Devereaux. Not even Shann, and she'd thought he was . . . She pulled her thoughts away from Shann.

Bligh took her arm as they walked down the narrow staircase, his hand still warm on her elbow as they crossed to the car, Shann's Alfa, and he settled her into the passenger seat before taking the wheel. The short drive home seemed to pass in a flash and now that the evening was over she wished silently again that it could have gone on for ever.

Kezia's mouth was dry and once or twice along the drive home she had to blink back sudden unaccountable tears. Bligh himself seemed loath to talk, his profile set and unapproachable, a frown on his brow.

They turned into the narrow gateway to Kezia's

house, and as the car bumped over the cattle grid she shot a startled look at him in the pale moonlit interior of the car. He would kiss her goodnight . . . She had a nerve-honing recollection of their exchange on the raft at the beach and her lips trembled, wanting and yet afraid.

He's a tourist, she reminded herself rather belatedly. He's a man on holiday, out for a good time, she repeated to herself. To him she was only a passing fling to entertain him while he was away from home. And he could even be married for all she knew, with a family—she pictured a dark-haired little boy in Bligh's image, and maybe a little girl, and she cringed inside, feeling cheap and nasty.

Of course he isn't married, she told herself, he would have said something. Don't be naïve, jeered another voice. You saw yourself how cagey he was about discussing his life. Don't be a fool, he'll only use you. Her stomach churned nauseously.

Devereaux dimmed the headlights as he turned in front of the house. Both Chris's mini-van and her mother's small sedan were parked in front, but they were obviously in bed, for the house was in darkness.

Reaching out slowly, Bligh switched off the ignition, plunging them into a far from peaceful silence. The air in the confines of the car grew thick and combustible, and Kezia turned nervously and held out her hand.

'Thank you for the lovely evening.' Her voice was thin and high as she watched the blurred outline of his features in the semi-moonlit interior of the car.

His hand took hers, holding it firmly. 'It was my pleasure, Kezia.'

His voice, low and molten, flowed out to surround her in a web of liquid silk and she felt her whole body grow hot, glad of the disguising semi-darkness. For the life of her she couldn't think of a word to say, even had her throat not been constricted with her increasing awareness of him and his potent attractiveness.

He moved his thumb gently over the back of her hand. 'My pleasure indeed.' His voice dropped even lower and still holding her hand he compelled her closer until his lips touched hers.

Kezia drew back as though she'd been burned. It was such exquisite, perilous pleasure. But if she let him kiss her she knew she would have absolutely no defence at all against his undeniable experience.

Momentarily his fingers tightened on the hand he continued to hold and her heart skipped a racing beat as she sensed he was about to press his advantage. Then she heard him sigh raggedly and his fingers slowly relaxed.

'Goodnight, Kezia. Sweet dreams.'

He released her hand and she just as suddenly wanted to lean closer to him, feel his arms about her, hear the safe thud of his heart beneath her cheek. At the perfidiousness of her reaction her shaking fingers fumbled with the door lock and she had to hold herself in check lest she scramble clumsily from the car. As it was, her handbag slid to the ground as she climbed out of the car and she had to grope around to find it before she whispered a mortified goodnight and hurried into the house.

Once inside she leant weakly back against the closed door, her knees quivering, long after the sound of the Alfa had faded away along the road. What a fool she was, running from him like a scared rabbit. For that was what she had been, she told herself, an inexperienced, gauche, unsophisticated, frightened rabbit. Chris was right: Bligh Devereaux was out of her league.

Pushing herself away from the door, she walked shakily along to her room and quickly undressed. Sliding beneath the cool sheets, she fought down the urge to drag the covers over her head and make it all go away.

So much for the new grown-up sophisticate. Kezia McCoy, woman of the world, a naïve twenty-year-old virgin out to gain a bit of experience. She cringed as she taunted herself. One tiny faltering footstep into Bligh Devereaux's world and she'd folded and run. She squeezed her eyes tightly closed in an effort to block out her self-derision.

'Good morning, Mr Devereaux.'

Kezia's head came up from the accounts she was doing at her desk in the office as her mother spoke into the telephone, and a dull flush washed her face. For the past three days, since the night Bligh had taken her out to dinner, she had been wallowing in a fit of depression. When she wasn't angrily chastising herself, that was. She recognised that her anger at her self-embarrassment was primarily at the root of her dejection.

She had been unforgivably foolish. What had been so terrifying about sharing an evening with a nice-looking man? She was twenty years old, for heaven's sake, not a child, she berated herself again. So a man expected a goodnight kiss! What was wrong with that? It was no reason to bolt like a startled colt. And after the way she'd behaved towards him to get back at Shann and Raewyn who could blame Bligh Devereaux for thinking the very worst of her? She had flirted with him, given him every indication that she fancied him.

And then she stumbled from his car like some panic-stricken schoolgirl way out of her depth. How she must have amused him! The way she amused everyone else, she reminded herself.

Poor little Kezia, who just hasn't grown up! Firstly she amuses everyone with her so transparent crush on Shann Evans and now she's managed to turn a simple goodnight kiss into ... Her cheeks grew suddenly feverishly hot as she remembered the sensational pressure of Bligh's lips on her own. No! she screamed angrily inside herself. It wasn't anything special. It was just a simple kiss.

'It's quite a bit of luck for the boat to arrive while you're here, isn't it?' Allie McCoy was saying. 'A lot of tourists miss seeing them and it is interesting to watch.'

Kezia stood up and replaced the large account file on the shelf behind her, then began to absently straighten the piles of invoices on the desktop, refusing to allow her gaze to stray towards her mother although no matter how hard she tried she couldn't block out her mother's voice.

'But of course it wouldn't be any trouble,' her mother was saying. 'It would be a pity if you missed seeing it. Look, I've just had a thought. If you don't mind driving down in the utility Kezia can pick you up on her way through. We have a container to collect and she'll be off down to collect it in a few minutes.'

The sheaf of invoices in Kezia's hand fell to the desk in disarray as she spun around to face her mother, shaking her head vigorously at her mother's suggestion.

Allie McCoy frowned at Kezia and after a few words of farewell, replaced the receiver.

'Oh, Mum, no!' Kezia burst out. 'I don't want to take Bligh Devereaux anywhere. I can't ... I can't ...' She stopped. She couldn't face him, but how could she tell her mother that without going into long self-damning explanations?

'What's wrong, love? I thought you rather liked him.' Allie crossed the office to her daughter. 'He wanted to order the taxi to take him down to Cascade and I thought since you were going down there anyway you wouldn't mind taking him along.'

'I ... It's not that ... I just ... Mum, can't you take him?' she appealed.

'Kezia, what's all this about?' Allie put her hand on her daughter's arm. 'It's not like you. Come to think of it, you've been overly quiet ever since the night you went out with Bligh Devereaux.' She looked sharply into her daughter's pale face. 'Didn't you enjoy the evening with him?' she asked softly after a slight pause.

'Yes, I enjoyed the evening,' Kezia replied quickly. 'But ...'

'But what?' prompted her mother.

'I just don't want to ...' she sighed, and shrugged, her eyes not meeting her mother's.

'Did he make a pass at you?' Allie asked.

'A pass?' Kezia repeated, flushing again.

'A pass.' Allie smiled. 'Or what is it Chris calls it? Did he put the hard word on you?'

'Mother!' Kezia gazed at her in horror and seeing her mother's teasing smile she felt herself reluctantly smile with her before they both broke into laughter, and Kezia wrinkled her nose. 'No, he didn't put the hard word on me. Not exactly.'

Allie McCoy's eyebrows rose enquiringly.

'Well, he did kiss me, but ...' Kezia shifted in embarrassment. 'Oh, Mum, I made a fool of myself with him. I didn't exactly give him the chance to make a pass at me—I kind of ran.'

'And now you feel naïve and foolish,' finished Allie, and Kezia nodded.

Her mother slipped her arm around Kezia's shoulders and gave her a squeeze. 'Don't be, love. If you didn't want to kiss him—well, he'll just have to accept that.'

At her mother's words Kezia felt even more of a fraud. If only it had been that simple and she hadn't wanted to kiss him. That was what was really eating away at her. She'd wanted him to kiss her all too much. And she knew instinctively that to invite Bligh Devereaux's kisses would have had her floundering out of control.

'So simply go and take him down to Cascade with you to watch the lighters at work. Just be your usual self,' advised her mother.

'I'm not sure I can.'

'Of course you can,' Allie grinned. 'He'll have to learn to live with the fact that he can't turn the heads of the McCoy women,' she teased, and Kezia found herself smiling.

'All right. I guess I could think of it as something like a visit to the dentist,' she grimaced. 'It will only hurt for a moment.'

But as she drew the utility to a halt in front of Cascade Court to find Bligh standing at the entrance waiting for her Kezia almost laughed hysterically at that statement. A moment had nothing to do with it, the moments were going to run together, one on top of the other.

He was dressed with easy casualness that in no way decried the fact that he was a man of some substance. His mid-blue scrub denims were tailored to hug his muscular thighs and the matching short-sleeved fitted shirt sat over his narrow hips, the top studs undone at the neck displaying a flash of fine dark hair on his chest as he came down the steps towards her. The early morning sunlight caught in the darkness of his hair as it lifted in the breeze, and Kezia thought the tightness in her throat would choke her.

Never in her life had she reacted so physically to a man the way she was responding to Devereaux. Not even Shann Evans had evoked such feelings inside her. By comparison her feelings for Shann had been empty, paltry things. But Bligh Devereaux was a stranger, a tourist who could be out for a good time. She barely knew him. And he was a mainlander.

'Morning, Kezia.' He slid on to the bench seat beside her and his smile made her heart flip over in her breast.

'Hello,' she managed a little breathlessly as a jumble of thoughts spun in a kaleidoscope as she turned back to the utility. Could it possibly be that she was in love with this handsome mainlander? Surely not? To her mortification she ground the gears as she shoved the lever in her agitation.

He made no comment, although she half expected one, and silence hung between them until they were on the roadway again and heading towards Cascade Bay.

'I'm glad I'm getting the chance to see the unloading of the supply ship while I'm here,' he said at last.

'Yes.' Kezia's voice seemed to echo inside her head

and her fingers flexed tightly on the steering wheel. She forced herself to draw a steadying breath. 'And you can get an elevated view here at Cascade,' she made herself speak naturally, although it cost her greatly. 'They'll be unloading at Cascade because the seas are a little rough around the Kingston jetty. The waters aren't deep enough for the ships to come right in, unfortunately, so they have to anchor offshore and the lighters do the unloading.'

'Everything comes in by lighter, even the vehicles?' he asked.

'That's right. Apart from the small amount that's air-freighted in. The lighters are virtually large rowboats, and the cars sit in the bottom and the boat gets towed to shore. Of course, with the larger vehicles such as tour buses, they lash two lighters together and bring the buses in straddled across them.

Just at that moment Kezia slowed as the road snaked in a sharp turn around a steep hillside and the large white supply ship sat on the deep mirror of blue water framed by the V-shape of two green striated hills. Even from this distance a seemingly tiny crane swung a matchbox sized tractor over the side of the New Zealand ship and set it unceremoniously in the bottom of a waiting lighter to be powered in to the jetty.

By the time Kezia had stopped the utility on the grassy verge overlooking the bay the same tractor was safely on shore. Bligh Devereaux regarded the proceedings with interest, and Kezia couldn't stop herself watching him. And as her eyes roved over him her whole body tensed with the yearning to reach out and touch him, to prove to herself that he was real, tangible, and not some mythical being she had conjured up to resurrect her bruised heart.

'I'm not holding you up, am I?' He turned back to her and his eyes were as blue as the morning sky.

'Oh no, not at all.' She knew she was blushing and took herself sternly to task. 'One of the boys will give me a wave when they get to ours,' she added hurriedly. 'We're only expecting one crate, some spare parts for the cars.'

His eyes watched her openly, the dark golden-tipped curls dancing in the breeze, her small slightly upturned nose with its dusting of light freckles, her large brown eyes fringed by dark lashes, the rosy flush that coloured the strong line of her high cheekbones, her lips, naturally red, curving generously, and her firm little chin.

Kezia's blush deepened and the tip of her tongue moistened her suddenly dry lips, drawing his attention back to them. Nerves fluttered in the pit of her stomach and she caught her breath raggedly in her chest.

Almost desperately she dragged her eyes from his and searched the jetty for some sign that they wanted her to collect her container. When one of the lighterage workers waved his arm and pointed to the ship her legs almost gave way beneath her with relief.

'The next one's mine,' she said unevenly, and climbed thankfully into the cab.

Without a word Devereaux slid in beside her and they drove down to the jetty where Kezia backed the utility up to the derrick and climbed out to watch as the large crate swung upwards and across and was set neatly on the tray of the utility.

Bligh walked around to join her and that same current of electricity glowed between them with such brilliance that Kezia was sure the other people around them must notice, and she shivered with nervousness.

'I think I'll stay down here for a while,' he said, his eyes half closed against the sun, shielding his expression. 'No doubt you have to get back.'

'Well, yes, I should.' Kezia moved backwards, tried to put more breathing space between them. 'Shall I . . . would you like me to call back for you later?'

He shook his head. 'No, don't worry. I'll get a lift with someone.' He had turned slightly away, seemed now to be giving all his attention to the movements of the men on the jetty as they went about their business with casual competence.

'Okay.' Kezia climbed into the truck and Bligh closed the door.

'Thanks for the lift down,' he said, but he had turned away before she could reply.

Taking the utility slowly up the hill, Kezia felt just a little deflated that he had chosen to remain on the jetty instead of returning with her, and she bit off an angry self-derisive retort. What was she so let down over? When she was with him she shook like a lily-livered shrinking violet, so why not be thankful that she had escaped from the tentacles of his apparent magnetism?

But still the flatness persisted and she wondered worriedly what could be the matter with her. She didn't seem to know herself any more. And the same feeling stayed with her until she forced herself to give her entire concentration to unpacking the car parts, checking invoices and moving the components into the storeroom.

On the surface at least she had put Bligh Devereaux from her mind all afternoon, but when she climbed tiredly into bed that night his face sprang back into her mind's focus with such swift vividness that it took her completely by surprise. With her defences down that one brief glimpse, a frame stopped out of a thousand frames, had a devastating effect on her. Her mind ruthlessly flashed back—to the pressure of his strong hand holding hers. His muscular body moved with hers to the beat of the music, the softness of her breast against the smoothness of his shirt taut across the breadth of his chest, the hardness of his thighs burning through the cotton of her skirt. And his lips on hers, firm, sensuous, demanding, tasting of the sea, a kiss that awakened a part of her that had been sleeping, as though she had been waiting just for him.

Kezia's fingers clutched the sheets and she squeezed her eyes tightly closed. It was all wrong. She couldn't feel this way about a man a virtual stranger she had known for only days, when for most of her life she had been so sure she loved Shann.

Shann. No, she hadn't loved Shann Evans. She had been in love with an idol she had created in her mind, crediting Shann with the qualities she had wanted him to have. And if it hadn't been for the arrival of Bligh Devereaux she would have gone on thinking she was in love with the image she had made of Shann.

She tossed restlessly. It was all so confusing. She wished she could wipe it from her thoughts. And what exactly was Bligh Devereaux's importance to Shann? Whenever Bligh appeared Shann was all nervous deference, like a man trying desperately to please his superior. Yet there was no reason for Shann to be like that. He ran the Court singlehandedly and it was one of the most successful complexes on the island. Why should he feel he needed to prove anything to the other man?

Unless ... Kezia frowned worriedly. No, it was ludicrous to even think it. Shann couldn't possibly be in financial difficulties. But her mother had asked her whether he had spoken about things at the motel. No—Kezia forced it from her mind. She was probably imagining it all. This whole episode with Bligh had thrown her completely off centre and she was beginning to imagine all sorts of crazy things. Like being in love with him. It was so far out it was almost funny, and she turned into a more comfortable position and settled down to sleep.

However, her soul-searching seemed to thresh about in her subconscious, because at regular intervals throughout the night she dozed and awoke, the same questions doggedly torturing her mind. Could she really be in love with Bligh Devereaux? Was this burning ache inside her for the touch of this handsome mainlander really love? A love that would endure the way the feeling her parents had had for each other had endured, living on with her mother just as strongly since her father's death four years earlier? For she knew she couldn't consider anything less. And if she was in love with Bligh, how could she possibly feel this way about him so soon when her whole young life had evolved, starry-eyed, around Shann Evans?

She brought Shann's attractive face into her mind, but it kept fading, Shann's familiar features giving way to the strong planes of Bligh's firm square jaw, straight nose, those watching, all-seeing eyes, his dark hair. And his lips. Lips that moved easily upwards at the corners into the earth-shattering smile that created so much havoc with her, that evoked such exquisite pleasure, such a shattering response when they touched hers.

The bed was suddenly a confinement, and Kezia sat up and ran her fingers distractedly through her hair. As her eyes became adjusted to the darkness it seemed that the walls of her room began to close in on her and she threw back the sheets and jumped out of bed. Leaning on her hands on the windowsill, she drew a few deep calming breaths, and her eyes caught the flicker of the light on the navigational beacon on Mount Pitt.

Not giving herself time to quell the idea that flooded her tortured mind, she hurriedly donned her pale blue fleecy cotton track suit and quietly opening her bedroom door she tiptoed through the hall and out the front door. Sitting on the bottom step, she slipped into her sneakers and then walked across to her motorcycle, running alongside it as she pushed it silently out on to the road, not starting the engine until she was out of earshot of the house.

She pulled the hood of her track suit top over her head and tied the gathering cord under her chin before riding slowly along in the darkness. The cool wind tugged at her clothing and whipped colour into her cheeks, banishing the heaviness of her broken night.

If she hurried she would be in time to see the dawn break over the ocean, and she accelerated a little as she began the wind up to the top of Mount Pitt. Many times over the years she had sat on top of the mountain gazing in wonder as the sun climbed into the sky, and no matter how heavy her heart was the spectacle always managed to lift her spirits, find her equilibrium again. Her parents had brought her up here one morning when she had been a very small child, and each time she sat watching she felt no less awe than she had at that first sunrise.

When she reached the top she switched off the engine and rocked the bike on to its stand, hurrying surefootedly up the grassy mound to sit on the cement seat and watch the well-known splendour, pushing her hood back so that the wind could thread through her dark curls, lifting them, lightening her troubled mind.

The glow of lightness had already begun to wash the horizon and she shivered, drawing her feet up and resting her chin on her knees, clasping her arms around her legs. A rapturous sigh escaped her lips, to be carried away on the breeze. Being up here, a very small part of a huge whole, watching the magnificent awakening, filled her with a reverence she couldn't begin to describe, for surely, she thought once again, this must be the very closest place to heaven she could ever imagine finding.

When he sat down beside her she accepted his presence without question. She should have been taken aback, surprised at least, for his rubber-soled shoes had made no sound as he approached, but she felt only a rightness that he should be here to share this moment with her, that he should be the first person to have done so. She felt him beside her, close but not actually touching her, one leg drawn up and the other stretched out in front of him as he relaxed, leaning on his elbows on the back of the seat.

It was quite light before Kezia broke the silence to speak.

'Doesn't it defy description?' she breathed, afraid to break the spell of wonderment, and led go of her drawn-up legs and turned towards him, the new-born sunshine highlighting the curve of her cheek, sparkling in the tips of each tossled curl.

'That's for sure,' he said, his voice deeply husky, his eyes not moving from her face.

'I've lost count of the number of times I've been up her to watch it.' She sighed again and took a deep breath. 'Mmm, everything smells so clean and fresh!' She laughed softly. 'I was just thinking that this must be the closest we could get to imagining heaven—and do you know, geographically speaking, it just about is the closest place to heaven you can get to on the island—I mean, Mount Bates is really about ten feet higher but it's a little more difficult to reach it's top and it's not cleared like this is, making you feel like you're on a tiny plateau looking down on earth.'

She turned towards him again, still easy with him, for some reason her shyness and uncertainty gone. 'In all the times I've come up here, even when I used to sneak up as a child, I've never seen a single soul. Whatever made you come up here this morning?'

He shrugged and leaned forward to rest his elbows on his knees, seemingly a little reluctant to take his eyes from her face. 'I woke up early and I couldn't seem to get back to sleep, and it just occurred to me as I lay there, so I came out before I could change my mind.'

'I couldn't sleep either,' Kezia said softly, and turned away to gaze out to sea, not wanting him to see the blaze of love she knew shone for him in her eyes. 'How did you get here?' she asked at last. 'I didn't notice a car. You didn't walk, did you?' she laughed.

'I started out to run, but I have to admit I walked part of the way.' One corner of his mouth lifted in amusement. 'I didn't realise how out of condition I was!'

Kezia was looking at him in amazement.

'I used to do a lot of long-distance running when I was at university and I've trained a little on and off over the years.' He smiled again. 'More off than on this last year or so! When I got to the top I flopped. I was around the front there lying on the grass getting my breath back when I heard your bike. And now I've recovered my breath, in a manner of speaking, I can say it's been worth it.' His eyes held hers again and a glow of pleasure fanned inside her.

Her night of sleeplessness, of churning everything over, torturing herself, faded away and it all became so very clear. It wasn't too soon; it never had been. Time had nothing to do with it. So she had known him for less than a week. So what? It only took a second. A look. A smile. This flame that burned inside her was for Bligh Devereaux and for him alone. She loved him, and it needed no soul-searching to tell her that. It was all so beautifully crystal clear.

He shook his dark head almost imperceptibly. 'Kezia.' Her name came out low and ragged and was stolen by the wind. Reaching out, he gently touched a dark curl of her hair, letting its softness twist around his finger before he let the finger slide sensuously along the line of her jaw to touch her lips.

'Heaven for sure,' he murmured as his lips came down to claim hers in a caress so gentle she had to swallow a lump that rose in her throat and blink back the rush of tears to her eyes.

His mouth moved lightly, arousingly on hers until her response changed the timbre of his kisses, firing them both with the searing flame of desire. Kezia's lips parted and his lips teased, tantalised, drew from her a reciprocating fire that frightened her yet held her bound to him. His arms were wrapped around her locking her against him, and when he finally surrendered her lips they were both breathless.

Resting his cheek, cold from the wind, against her forehead, Bligh held her closely for an eternity or an instant while their heartbeats hammered in unison. Eventually he raised his head to look down at her face, his eyes still lit by the fire of their arousal.

'Kezia McCoy,' he said huskily, 'if you're a dream, some mythical wraith of the dawn, then now that I've found you promise me you're not going to fade away on me.'

'I'm real enough,' she said, her voice filled with a silky sensuousness that made him draw a ragged breath, his hands sliding around to cup her face, his eyes seeming to devour her, as though he was committing each feature to memory.

He drew a steadying breath, and his jaw tensed as he fought to control the desire that burned in the depths of his eyes and he smiled slowly. 'The real McCoy?' he said unevenly, then grimaced. 'Sorry about that, Kez. Put it down to the fact that you've knocked me for six, my very real Kezia McCoy.'

His fingers caressed her face, her earlobes, before he slid his arms around her again and hugged her to him, one hand moving in the darkness of her hair. His sweat-shirt was warm and smooth against her skin and beneath her cheek she could feel the strong thudding of his heart, the musky maleness of him tantalising her nostrils.

'Oh, Kez, you're just like the new dawn to me,' he murmured so quietly that she had to strain to catch his words. 'A breath of fresh air in the cloying commotion of my life and I'd like to stop the world here and now before . . .' His voice faded away and his arms tightened around her for a moment. Then he was holding her away from him and he kissed her gently on the tip of her nose.

'Come on, Kezia McCoy,' he said lightly, in command of himself now, drawing her to her feet. 'Let's go back down to earth while we're still able, if you'd be so kind as to share your motorcycle with a humble mainlander.'

He smiled down at her, and Kezia would have granted him anything within her power, her heart soaring high as an eagle, swelling wondrously with love for him.

And she walked on air all morning after she had dropped him at the gates of Cascade Court and watched his tall figure disappear around the drive before she turned the motorcycle towards home. She pottered happily about the house, cleaning and tidying, humming happily to herself, clutching the newness of her love to her as she prepared plates of fresh crisp salad and ripe Pilhi bananas for the family's lunch. Her mother and brothers arrived home together, and they couldn't help but notice the glow in her eyes.

'You look like the cat who's swallowed the canary,' remarked Chris, starting on his lunch. 'What've you been up to, Sis?'

'Nothing.' Kezia smiled. 'It's just such a lovely day, don't you think?'

'Looks just like yesterday to me,' said Toby, making a point of glancing out of the kitchen window. 'It's all right for you, Kezia, I've only got nine days left of my school holidays and then it's back to the saltmines for me.'

'Best days of your life, kid,' teased Chris. 'Wait till you have to get out into the big world and earn a living!'

'Amazing!' Kezia joined in. 'The way he talks you'd think he knew all about it, wouldn't you?'

They continued on in a lighthearted vein until Kezia began to stack their plates on the sink.

'Got any plans for this afternoon, love?' asked her mother, getting up to start washing the dishes.

'Not really,' Kezia shrugged, her mind going to Bligh, and she smiled secretly. 'I might do a bit of shopping and call down at Cascade Court.'

Chris looked up from the last of his homemade apple pie. 'Don't bother, Kez. Shann's not there.'

'Oh, isn't he?' she caught herself before she told them she hadn't been thinking of Shann.

'No. He left an hour or so ago,' said Chris.

'Left? What, on the plane, you mean?' she said in surprise.

'Mmm. He's gone to Sydney.' Chris brought his empty plate over and handed it to his mother. 'With that guy you had dinner with the other night. What's his name? Devereaux.'

CHAPTER SIX

Two weeks later Kezia admitted to herself that the numbing pain she had felt when Chris had so innocently dropped his bombshell hadn't faded one fraction. In her hurt and disillusionment she screamed at herself to forget Bligh Devereaux, to stop this masochistic urge that allowed her to think about him when the remembering brought such emotional and physical distress.

Yet when she played that scene on the top of Mount Pitt over in her mind, each precious moment an agonising memory, she knew that Bligh had not really committed himself in any way, while she had mistakenly believed that the moment hadn't needed words, that they had been tuned to the very same wavelength, had been hearing the same melody.

So it seemed that Raewyn was right, she was naïve and unsophisticated and . . . and every other adjective you could imagine. And it all added up to one thing: Kezia McCoy, inexperienced little virgin.

And Bligh Devereaux. What had it all meant to him? Were Shann and Chris right all along in warning her off the handsome mainlander? Did Bligh see it as a holiday fling, a brief interlude, quite pleasant, but not one to disrupt the even flow of his world? Certainly it hadn't meant enough to him to prevent his return home to whatever awaited him there. Or whoever waited there, she reminded herself with brutal honesty.

Within a week the strain of pretending an indifference, playing a part in front of her family, had begun to tell on Kezia, and as the day drew near for Toby's return to boarding school in Brisbane their mother firmly insisted that Kezia accompany him and have the short holiday she had suggested. Kezia resisted, of course, but her mother was adamant, for even Kezia herself couldn't fail to see the paleness of her face and the dark circles of tiredness under her eyes.

Now here she was sitting staring at the telephone in her aunt's house in suburban Brisbane with two telephone numbers on the notepad in front of her, numbers listed against Devereaux, B. If she spoke to him here on his own ground she would know by his tone if she had read too much into his kisses and caresses.

She picked up the receiver and listened to the dial tone for a moment before hurriedly replacing the instrument on its cradle. What if he thought she was chasing him? Men hated that. How often had she seen Chris waving his hands frantically at their mother when certain girls phoned him up? 'Tell her I've joined the Foreign Legion, or donated my body to science. Tell her anything!' Chris had whispered urgently.

It took her five minutes to convince herself that calling him up to say hello as she was in Brisbane wasn't chasing him. And they were five precious minutes, she told herself exasperatedly, because her aunt and uncle would be home in less than half an hour. Not that she was being underhanded about using the telephone. She just wanted privacy for the call.

When the first B. Devereaux turned out to be a middle-aged lady who denied any knowledge of a Bligh in her family Kezia felt almost ill with a mixture of relief and regret as she apologised and shakily broke the connection.

The other number was a B. Devereaux in the suburb of Kenmore, and Kezia put the call through before she lost her nerve. The ringing tone continued until she very nearly hung up.

'Hello.' The feminine voice, sounding quite young, came breathlessly over the line, as though the girl had had to run to answer the phone.

'Good morning. Would Mr Bligh Devereaux be there, please?' Kezia asked quickly, her heart thudding noisily in her ears.

'Bligh? No, sorry, he isn't. He's working, as usual,' came the voice.

'Oh, I see. Well, I'm sorry for bothering you,' Kezia began.

'That's okay. This is Dale Devereaux. Can I give Bligh a message?'

Kezia thought her heart had stopped. 'No,' she said quickly. 'No, thanks. I'll ring back later. Goodbye.' She dropped the receiver as though it was burning hot.

After a few minutes the numbness began to wear off and she felt a tiny pain around her heart claw at her and grow in intensity. So now she knew. He had been married all along. And the woman, his wife, Dale Devereaux, had sounded nice and friendly. Kezia experienced a terrible guilt, knowing how she would have felt if she found out her husband had been involved with another woman. Almost involved, to be fair.

Well, that was that. He was married, had had no right to kiss her. The pain clutching her heart took her breath away, leaving a throbbing ache that she knew was going to remain with her for some time. And it hurt so much more than anything had hurt before. Even when she had found out about Shann and Raewyn.

Kezia walked slowly back to her room. She would just have to put Bligh Devereaux out of her mind. For her aunt's and uncle's sakes she would have to make some pretence of enjoying the remainder of her holiday here in Queensland, and then she would return to her life on Norfolk Island, engross herself in her work, forget the handsome mainlander who had had such a devastating effect on her.

She sank down on the edge of her bed. Her heart felt heavy, and of their own accord tears blurred her vision and one lonely droplet flowed over and trickled slowly down her cheek.

'Kez, love, have you seen this advert in the paper?' her uncle Joe was sitting back at the kitchen table as Kezia and her aunt cleared away the breakfast dishes and began washing up. 'Cascade Court, Norfolk Island. Isn't that young Evans' place?'

'Cascade Court? Yes, that's Shann's. What's the matter with it?' Kezia walked around to glance over her uncle's shoulder. The word 'auction' sprang off the page and literally drove the air from her body, leaving her with the distinct impression that she was going to faint. Her eyes ran over the newsprint in disbelief.

The half-page advertisement was headed 'South Pacific Island Resort. Cascade Court Hotel-Motel, just over three hours from Brisbane.' There must be some mistake. There had to be. Kezia's eyes went to the pen sketch of the complex. There was no mistaking the distinctive V-shape of the building of the Court. It couldn't be any other motel.

Her eyes raced over the page. 'One of the largest tourist resort complexes on Norfolk Island, set on approximately six and a half acres of tropical beauty right near the island's duty free shopping with lots of room for future expansion. This is a rare opportunity for investment. Turnover for the last twelve months eight hundred and fifty thousand dollars.'

Expelling the breath she was holding, Kezia shook her head. 'It can't be,' she said, unaware that she had spoken. 'Not the Court. It's Shann's life!'

'Wonder why he's selling,' remarked her uncle. 'Could have got himself into financial difficulties, I guess.'

'But Shann wasn't having any money worries,' Kezia began, and then recalled again her mother's questions about the motel. 'Everything was going well,' she added to convince herself, 'he told me so just a few weeks ago.'

'I didn't know the islanders could sell their businesses just like that,' put in her aunt.

'They can't. To begin with we have to offer the sale to other islanders before putting it on an open market.' Kezia frowned. 'But the sort of money Shann would want for the Court—well ...' she stopped and returned her gaze to the newspaper her uncle had laid out on the table. 'The auction's on Wednesday in the city. I just can't believe it!'

'This Shann Evans, he's James Evans' son, isn't he?' asked her aunt, and Kezia nodded. 'I thought he was a friend of Chris's.'

'He is,' Kezia told her.

'Then why wouldn't he have mentioned selling the motel? It must have been in the wind for some time, surely.'

'I don't know,' Kezia said softly. She would have thought Shann would have told Chris at least, and if Chris had known wouldn't he have told her?

'Are you going to go? To the auction sale, I mean?' Her aunt's words brought Kezia back to the present.

'I think I will,' she said slowly. It was Shann's motel, so he would be there, and she could ask him why he was selling out, giving up all that he'd worked for, all that his father had built up for him.

On Wednesday, after a strained six days of waiting, Kezia walked nervously into the multi-storied building in Elizabeth Street and glanced at the list of offices for the name of the real estate agency handling the auction sale of Shann's motel.

She had telephoned her mother, and Allie McCoy had only found out herself about Shann's intention to sell Cascade Court a few days after Kezia left. She told Kezia that the island was agog with the news, with every one speculating about Shann's reason for selling and on the eventual buyer. Of course, no one was pleased, but Kezia had no time to go into any detail. Her mother told her Shann had returned to the island but had left for the mainland again.

As the lift whirred eerily upwards with disorientating speed Kezia very nearly lost all inclination to attend the sale. The doors slid noiselessly open and her nerve almost failed her. Had there not been two people waiting to take the elevator down she knew she would not have stepped out into the plushly carpeted foyer. But she could hardly stand there looking like a pale statue and she forced herself to move, to stride up to the open double doors of the auction room.

An attractive girl standing by the door smiled at Kezia and handed her a glossy pamphlet. As she slipped into the room Kezia's eyes searched quickly for Shann's familiar face, but he wasn't among the ten or so people already present.

The auction room was set out rather like a lecture room with a table out in front of rows of identical black chairs. On the pegboards set up to one side were various papers and photographs relating to Cascade Court, while in the centre a video outfit was running a colour film taken on the island around about the motel.

Kezia walked across and ran her eyes over the neatly set out sheets. There was a floor plan of the buildings, a site plan, a photocopy of the full title deeds, an inventory that included everything from alcohol to pot plants, approximately six foolscap pages of the form of contract, a profit and loss statement, all interspersed with vivid, coloured photographs of the interior and exterior of the complex.

Slowly Kezia returned to the very back row of seats and sat down, flipping through the glossy brochure, her eyes not seeing any of it. This must all surely be a dream. Shann would never consider selling out—the Court was his life. But there was no way that the sketches, the photographs, could be of any other business on the island.

The room began to fill up, mainly with successful-looking men in conservative business suits, who nodded to each other. There was only a sprinkling of women, most appearing to be attending in secretarial capacities, and before long there was only standing room behind Kezia left, and this too was soon taken up.

Kezia searched the sea of suits for Shann, but he still hadn't put in an appearance by the time a tall middle-aged man walked up to the table out front and began to set out his papers. By the doorway to Kezia's left a group moved as several more chairs were passed in and set along the aisle.

What actually caught Kezia's eye at that moment she couldn't later have told, but as the seats were taken a dark-headed figure reached over and secured one of the chairs for the very chic young woman standing by his side. Kezia's heartbeats stopped and started and raced erratically.

He was the last person she had expected to see here. But there was no mistaking his dark hair, the broad shoulders moulded by his light grey business suit, and as he turned slightly his virile profile took her breath away. The clarity with which she had recalled those strongly chiselled features frightened her, as though the sketch of those features had been drawn on her memory with an indelible pencil.

Bligh Devereaux leaned forward and put his hand on the girl's shoulder as she sat down in front of him, and she turned to smile up at him, her eyes bright. Her hand went up to cover his were it rested on the pale mulberry chiffon of her very feminine blouse. Kezia forced her eyes away from Bligh Devereaux to concentrate on the girl.

The shade of her lipstick on a bow-shaped mouth complemented the darker mulberry of her fashionable shirt and emphasised the whiteness of her small perfect teeth. Somehow the young woman matched her voice, and not for a moment did Kezia doubt that this was the Dale Devereaux who had answered her phone call. Her hair was long, falling in natural waves, and a lighter brown than Bligh's, and even from this distance Kezia could see the clear grey of the other girl's eyes.

Perhaps feeling Kezia's close scrutiny, Dale Devereaux looked across and their eyes met for a few seconds before Kezia's gaze fell away, the brief smile the other girl had given her filling her with a pang of painful guilt.

Kezia sank back in her seat. They made a nice-looking couple, Bligh Devereaux and his wife, Dale. Her eyes slid irresistibly back to Bligh's tall figure and the aching around her heart brought a lump to her throat. How could he have done it? Kissed her, caressed her, held her? While his wife waited at home unsuspecting. Or maybe they had a civilised relationship, each allowing the other such freedom.

Bligh moved his dark head and Kezia drew back behind the screen of the man beside her. She couldn't bear to test his reactions if he caught sight of her. Surprise? Guilt? Concern that she might make waves for him?

What could he possibly be here for anyway? she wondered, but before she could do more than form the question in her mind the auctioneer was clearing his throat and began to speak. With apologies he launched into the list of conditions of sale, a lot of which went over Kezia's head as she only half listened to the mention of vendors and purchasers, options and transfer of licence. It seemed to go on for ever, and Kezia kept her eyes on her hands clasped in her lap.

Eventually the tone of the auctioneer's voice changed and the room shuffled and sat up in seats as

one. The auctioneer assured them that he was
rendering a lucrative business on an island with a big
future, the area of the site offering room for expansion
in the way of tennis courts, sauna and suchlike.

'What offers?' he asked, his voice loudly business-
like. 'Can I get a start? Who'll give me a start?' His
eyes moved around the room.

'All right, Mr Auctioneer,' came a voice to Kezia's
right, 'I'll make it seven hundred.'

Kezia's eyes widened with shock. Seven hundred?
The Court was worth over a million!

'Thank you, sir,' said the auctioneer. 'That's seven
hundred thousand. 'I'm looking for fifty. At seven
hundred thousand. Who'll make it seven-fifty?'

Bids came from both sides of the room, although no
words were spoken by the bidders until the price of
nine hundred thousand dollars was reached and the
bids ceased.

'It's a way of life, ladies and gentlemen,' appealed
the auctioneer. 'A Pacific paradise. At nine hundred
it's a steal. At nine hundred thousand I'll call it once.'

The gavel hit the desk with a bang that made Kezia
jump.

'At nine hundred thousand I'll call it twice. At nine
hundred thousand I'll call it three times.' The
auctioneer seemed to sigh. 'That unfortunately is
below the reserve, sir,' he looked over to Kezia's left.
'I can't sell it here at that price, but we have the owner
on the telephone in the next office if you'd care to
discuss the price with us. Thank you for attending,
ladies and gentlemen.' He collected his papers
together as people slowly began to file out of the room.

The man beside Kezia moved and she hurriedly
followed him, keeping the milling crowd between

herself and Bligh Devereaux. She had every intention of fading out, fleeing without letting him know she had been there, seen him, and she might have succeeded but for the booming voice of a man behind her who hailed a friend standing near Bligh Devereaux. At the sound of the loud voice quite a few people turned towards them and fatefully the crowd opened up right in front of Kezia as she waited to file out of the room.

Blue eyes caught her, impaling her to the spot, although had she been capable of movement her escape was effectively blocked by the people in front of her. That same crowd didn't deter Bligh. He was beside her before she could command her seized muscles to break away.

'Kezia!' He caught her arm, the gently potent demand in his voice and the burning touch of his fingers reduced her knees to water and her heartbeats echoed inside her like the rattle of a kettledrum.

'Kezia,' he repeated, his voice a soft caress, and his smile . . .

She couldn't allow herself to think about his smile, for she knew how close that smile came to discomposing her completely.

'What are you doing here? I thought . . .?' he asked, then shook his head almost imperceptibly. 'No matter. You're here.' His voice dropped even further to the deep intimacy that struck all the right chords within her, her body seemingly tuned to his sound, his touch. 'Where are you staying?'

Her face had paled and she shivered uncontrollably as she stood looking up at him, unable to move, to find breath to answer him.

His smile faded just a little then and his lashes fell

over the brightness of his eyes as he waited for her to speak and the set of his lips seemed to take on a slight tightness.

Kezia swallowed, fighting the blurr of tears that blinded her, choked her, but by the time she had herself under some command again, would have spoken, the girl Dale Devereaux appeared at Bligh's shoulder.

'Bligh, they're waiting for you,' she said softly, her eyes taking in his hand where it had tightened on Kezia's arm.

Kezia searched worriedly for some sign of displeasure in the other girl's eyes, but strangely there was none, no suspicion, only a faint frown of enquiry, curiosity, perhaps.

'I'll be right there,' he said, his eyes not leaving Kezia's face. 'Kezia?'

Her eyes fell to his hand and he slowly released her.

'Bligh!' the young woman repeated, and the softly spoken word galvanised Kezia into action at last.

'I have to go,' she blurted out the words in an agitated rush. 'I . . . It's been nice seeing you again, Mr Devereaux. Goodbye.'

She turned and made a headlong dash from the auction room, jostling a couple of men who blocked the hallway. Passing the lift and the waiting throng, she tore down the steps, not stopping until she was out in Elizabeth Street, and only then did she pause momentarily to catch her breath before hurrying up towards the city centre and the anonymity of the crowds.

'Was it actually Cascade Court they were auctioning?' asked her uncle when she eventually returned to the house. She'd spent hours walking past shop windows, not seeing the merchandise displayed therein.

Kezia nodded. 'Yes, it was the Court. But Shann wasn't there.'

'Oh. Did it fetch a good sum?' asked her uncle. 'Seems to me it would be a valuable business.'

'It didn't reach the reserve price, so I don't know what happened. They'd probably have to negotiate, I guess. The last bid was nine hundred thousand dollars,' Kezia said flatly.

'Perhaps Shann won't sell then,' put in her aunt, 'not if he can't get his price, and nine hundred thousand is well below what it's worth, I would have thought.'

'Depends how much or how desperately he wants to sell out,' suggested her uncle. 'Now I've always found that when I'm buying the price is exorbitant and when I'm selling I have to hit bedrock,' he smiled ruefully. Any other remark he was about to make was cut off by the ringing of the telephone and Kezia crossed to answer it.

'Kezia!' His voice was an assault on her relaxed defences, and she drew a sharp breath.

CHAPTER SEVEN

THERE was no way he could know she was here. No way at all.

'I'm sorry, you have the wrong number.' Kezia replaced the receiver and turned back into the living room, but the phone jangled again before she could resume her seat.

'Shall I get it this time?' Her aunt made to stand up, but Kezia shook her head.

'Kezia, don't hang up!' Bligh said commandingly.

'I don't think you have the right person,' she began.

'I know I have the right person,' he said softly, a tinge of mockery in his voice.

Kezia stood speechless for a moment. 'How did you get my number?' she asked at last, her voice sounding low and unlike her own.

'From your mother,' he replied easily. 'Have dinner with me?'

'I'm sorry, I can't tonight,' she broke in.

He laughed softly. 'I can't tonight either—I'm tied up myself. I was about to suggest tomorrow night.'

'I'm sorry, I can't.' Kezia's fingers were white on the receiver.

'Then the night after that? Friday night?' he persisted, a slight edge to his voice.

'I'm ... I'm flying home that afternoon,' she said, grabbing at the first excuse she could think of.

There was a tense pause.

'Kezia, I want to see you.' His voice flowed about

her, an invisible web playing havoc with her sensitive nerve-ends. And for a moment she would have given in, taken him on any terms he wished to dictate, anything to feel his arms about her again, holding her against the strength of his thudding heartbeats. But his wife's face swam before her, cutting her like a knife's thrust, and she stiffened, wanting to cry out with the pain.

'I guess I don't want to see you,' she said then, her voice tight and forced, her heart aching, and she hoped she was inflicting just a little of her pain on him.

This time the silence was loud and long, stretching until she could no longer stand the strain. 'I have to go now. I'm sorry. Good . . . Goodbye.'

'I'm sorry too,' said Bligh without expression. 'But not goodbye. Au revoir.'

The dial tone buzzed in Kezia's ear and she dropped the receiver and stood looking at it, that same throbbing numbness suffusing her mind and body.

For some seconds she willed the phone to ring once more so that she could talk to him again, explain . . . But it didn't. It simply sat there smuggly silent, while she tried to tell herself it was all for the best. She wasn't the type of girl to indulge in affairs with married men, no matter how attractive, or how persuasive. Or how much she cared.

'Are you really going home the day after tomorrow?' her aunt asked sympathetically as Kezia sat down. 'I didn't mean to listen, love. I couldn't help but hear you.'

'Would you mind terribly if I did go home a few days early?' Kezia asked them.

'Of course not,' reassured her aunt. 'You do as you like. We don't mind at all.'

'I think I will, then.' Kezia fought a rush of tears. 'I
. . . Mum's been managing long enough without me
and she hasn't had a holiday herself yet,' she added,
feeling something of a fraud.

In actual fact there was a vacant seat, a late
cancellation, on the Norfolk Airlines plane the very
next day, so Kezia left Brisbane and flew back to the
island feeling rather like a wounded animal yearning
for the sanctuary of its lair to lick its wounds.

'We missed you,' smiled Allie McCoy as she passed
her daughter a cup of coffee. They were just finishing
their dinner on Kezia's first evening back.

'Sure did,' agreed Chris, spooning sugar into his
own coffee cup. 'The old place was like a mausoleum
without you.'

'That's an impressive word,' Kezia raised her
eyebrows. 'Have you been getting some culture since
I left?'

Chris grinned goodnaturedly. 'You could say that. I
met this neat little chick from Melbourne. She's on a
working holiday and she's just started housemaiding
up at the Hillcrest. What a body!' He kissed his
fingertips expressively. 'And on top of that she's got a
B.A. You know, Brains Also.'

Kezia laughed, feeling a rush of happiness to be
home again. 'Then what does she see in you? No one
in their right mind would take you on, Chris McCoy?'

'You don't appreciate my finer points, Kez,' he
said taking mock offence. 'Maybe she'll teach me
everything she knows.' He winked exaggeratedly as he
reached across the table for a large slice of passionfruit
tart.

'It can't be love, your appetite is still intact,' Kezia
teased him.

'Well, I can't say the same for you, Sis. You've hardly eaten anything. Don't tell me you're in love?' Chris bit into the delicious pie.

The smile on Kezia's face froze fractionally before she raised her coffee cup to her lips, taking a concentrated sip before giving a slightly forced laugh. 'Only with love, perhaps.' The joke sounded cynical even to herself, and her mother's eyes rested worriedly on her.

'By the way, did you hear from Bligh Devereaux while you were in Brisbane?' she asked her daughter. 'He rang up to speak to you while you were away, and when I told him you were with your aunt and uncle he got your number so he could look you up.'

'Yes, he did phone,' Kezia replied evenly, giving the tablecloth a lot of attention, 'but unfortunately I was coming home the only evening he was free, so that was bad luck.' She took another sip of her coffee her eyes on the dark liquid. 'Anyway, enough of this. What's been happening here while I've been away?' She forced a measure of enthusiasm into her voice.

'Nothing much,' remarked Chris. 'At least, nothing that anyone's noticed. Everyone's been so agog at Shann selling the Court that it's overshadowed everything else that's happened.'

'Did you go along to the auction sale, love?' Kezia's mother asked gently.

'Yes. But it was a bit of an anticlimax really.' Kezia kept her voice matter-of-fact, pushing those pain-filled moments with Devereaux to the furthest corner of her mind. 'People made their bids and then the bidding stopped below the reserve price. It was all over in minutes.'

'You mean no one bought it?' Chris asked

incredulously. 'But it's a goldmine! I wish we'd had the money.'

Kezia pulled a face at him. 'Where would we get that kind of money? It was passed in at nine hundred thousand dollars.'

'Maybe I could marry a rich widow, a millionairess,' he suggested.

'Pigs might fly, too!' Kezia had to smile at him.

'If no one offered enough money does that mean Shann didn't sell out after all?' asked their mother.

'I'm not sure,' Kezia frowned. 'The auctioneer invited the highest bidder to negotiate with Shann, so who knows?'

'Who was it, the highest bidder?' asked Chris . 'Did you see him?'

Kezia shook her head. 'They didn't even call out their bids after the initial one. It could have been any one of fifty well-dressed business-type men.'

'You mean they all had their secret signals, like touching their noses or winking their left eyes?' laughed Chris, highly amused.

'Must have been something like that.' Kezia drained her coffee cup. If she was honest she'd have to admit that she had been so full of seeing Devereaux that only part of her mind had been on the auction sale. And a small part at that. 'Have you . . . is Shann back yet?'

Chris and their mother exchanged a quick glance.

'No, not that I know of,' answered Allie McCoy. 'When he was back for those few days no one heard anything—nothing positive anyway. There were plenty of rumours and Shann didn't exactly make himself available for questioning.'

There was a heavy silence at the table that was

relieved by the insistent trilling of the telephone, and
Allie rose and left the room to answer it.

'Kez, about Shann.' Chris watched his finger trace
the abstract pattern on his coffee cup. 'How do you—
well, feel about him? Really?'

'Oh, Chris, what's that got to do with anything?'
Kezia parried his question with her own query.

'Look, I know you always had a bit of a crush on
him but—well——' he stopped as though he was
searching for the right words.

'I haven't still got a crush on him, if that's what's on
your mind.' She kept her voice light.

'That's not quite what I'm getting at, Kez. Did he
. . . has he said how he feels about you?'

'Made me aware of his intentions?' Kezia found some
amusement in her words, and she wondered rather
wryly if she was really as fickle about her feelings for
Shann as she appeared to be. Even in her own eyes it
appeared to be 'off with the old, on with the new'!

'Well, has he?' pressed Chris.

'We haven't discussed it. It would be pretty
pointless considering the thing he has going with
Raewyn Bourke, wouldn't you say?'

'You know about that?' Chris looked at her in part
surprise part concern. 'Did Shann tell you?'

'Not exactly. I suppose it was fairly obvious if you
wanted to see it.' She couldn't quite keep the memory
of those few moments when she'd overheard Raewyn
from adding an edge to her voice, it still flicked her on
her raw pride.

'I kind of tried to hint it to you once or twice, but I
figured you'd grow out of your crush.' Chris sighed.
'Hell, Kez, I never could understand why you were all
starry-eyed over him. What do you see in him?'

'Past tense, Chris, so don't worry about it any more.'

'I'm sorry, Kezia. But I have to say I'm glad. Shann's a friend but—well, he's not husband material. Not for you, anyway.'

Kezia's lips tightened. Not for an inexperienced little virgin like your sister, she finished for him. 'I'm not looking for a husband,' she began a trifle acidly, but was interrupted by her mother's return.

'That was Meg. She'll be coming back to work tomorrow. Her ankle's almost completely back to normal now.' Allie sat down and added more coffee to her cup. 'She says she heard Shann would be back at the end of the week.'

'He didn't sell out, then?' Chris shot a glance at his sister.

'No one knows for sure, Meg says. I guess we'll all have to wait and see.'

It was actually two weeks before Kezia saw Shann Evans. She had delivered a taxi fare, two new arrivals, from the airport to Cascade Court, and as she set the two lightweight suitcases by the reception desk and handed the couple over to the young receptionist, Shann strode from the direction of the restaurant across the foyer towards his office. At the sound of her call he turned around and smiled widely at her.

'Kezia! Hey, how are you? Have a nice holiday? Brisbane, wasn't it?'

'Yes, thanks.' She saw the nervous movement of his eyes as they didn't meet hers even as his mouth lifted in his charmingly familiar smile. 'Shann, can I talk to you for a minute?'

'Gee, Kez, I'm flat to the boards at the moment,' he made a show of glancing at his wristwatch.

'I won't hold you up for long,' she persisted.

'Okay. Come on along to the office.' He led her down the short hallway. 'Would you like something to drink? Coffee or tea?' Walking across to his desk, he began gathering together a sheaf of papers, his fingers nervously flipping over the pages.

'No, thanks. Shann, did you sell the Court?' Kezia came straight to the point.

'Look, Kez, I'm far too busy to chat . . .' he began.

'I don't want to chat with you, Shann. I just asked you a question that has a simple answer. Did you sell or not? Yes or no? It won't go any further if you'd rather it didn't.' She watched him frown down at the papers he held.

'Yes, I did sell out,' he replied at last with feeling. 'Does that satisfy your curiosity? Please yourself if you decide to put everyone's mind at rest. You'd have found out sooner than later, as it happens,' he finished a little less aggressively.

'But why? Did you have financial trouble?'

'No, I didn't,' he came back quickly. 'It's never been better, as a matter of fact.'

'You didn't even hint that you were thinking of selling. Not to me, or Chris, or anyone, and I can't understand that.' She watched him as he shifted irritatedly.

'Kez, this *is* my hotel. I have every right to do with it as I please,' he said with revived ire, throwing the papers back on the desk. 'I decided to sell it.'

'I know it's your hotel, but it's part of the island, and . . .'

'Oh, for heaven's sake, Kezia!' he broke in on her.

'I'm fed up to the back teeth with all that. I've just about eaten, slept, breathed it. That outlook's out of date, it's for the birds.' He took a couple of angry steps across the carpet and turned back towards her, hands on hips. 'This hotel is an inanimate object that provides food for my table, clothes for my back, and for that matter the island's only land to stand on. There are plenty of other pieces of dirt around the world that will do just as well.'

'Don't you feel anything at all for our heritage?' Kezia asked him softly.

'Heritage?' He laughed mockingly. 'What's so damn special about our heritage? Everyone has one. The mainlanders even flash theirs about every now and then when they get all patriotic. And when it all boils down to it what were they anyway? Just a mob of convicts. It's the same with us. We're all descended from a bunch of cut-throat mutineers who should have been hanged.'

'Shann!'

He stood rigidly and then sighed, pushing his dark hair back from his forehead. 'I'm sorry, Kezia—I shouldn't have said that, knowing how strongly you feel about it, but I just don't feel the same way. I want to live a little, see something of the world before I'm too old to enjoy it.'

'Surely you could do that without selling the Court? You could put in a manager,' she suggested.

Shann shook his head. 'I'm not used to travelling on a shoestring. To keep everything at the Court up to scratch a considerable amount of the profits have to go right back into the hotel, so . . .' He raised his hands and let them fall.

'But your father and his father built this place up

from nothing. For you. Don't you want to hand it on to your family?'

'I am my family,' he stated firmly. 'I don't like kids, Kez, and I somehow can't see myself as a doting daddy. Besides, by the time any kids I might have grow up they'd probably thank me for getting rid of the place. Believe me, hotel work is not the easy glamour it may look to be.'

Kezia watched him, his uneasy nervousness, the restlessness in his face, and knew a sadness for him, for what might have been.

Shann walked across to stand in front of her, his finger lifting her chin. 'Have I shattered all your childhood illusions about me, Kez?' he asked softly, his eyes settling on her lips.

'I told you before, Shann, I'm not a child any more. And I don't think I have any illusions left either. About you or anyone else,' she finished bitterly.

'Hey, do I detect a hint of an unhappy love affair?' he teased, all anger gone from him now he had the conversation back in hand. 'What's been going on while I was away?'

'Don't be ridiculous!' She tried to pull away from him, but his hands had fallen to her arms, holding her where she was.

'Maybe you met him in Brisbane,' he teased, and Kezia's face flamed. 'Well—a mainlander! I thought you didn't like mainlanders, Kezia McCoy?'

'I don't! And this is silly, Shann. Let me go. We weren't talking about me, we were discussing you and the hotel.' She shifted, but he continued to hold her easily captive.

'I'd much rather talk about you,' he said deeply, and

his lips had claimed hers before Kezia was even aware of his intention.

For a fraction of a second her surprises held her frozen. Her one coherent thought was that having Shann kiss her was the epitome of all her girlish dreams. But she wasn't a naïve girl any longer, and Shann's kisses repulsed rather than aroused, brought another handsome face, demandingly sensual lips, back with brutal suddenness, and she pushed her hands agitatedly against his shoulders, trying to break away from the constriction of his hold on her.

However, her struggles only seemed to inflame him even more, his kiss deepened, bruising her vulnerably soft mouth, and his hands were constraining bonds about her. He raised his head to plunder the softness of her throat and she drew a rasping breath.

'Shann, please . . .'

'Could I see you when you're free?' a cold voice asked from behind them, and Shann released her as they both started and turned together towards the open doorway.

At the sound of his voice a tiny bud of hope began to bloom inside her, that he had returned for her and . . . Hard blue steel raked the two of them and as his eyes met Kezia's she flinched under the impact of his so obvious displeasure. His presence alone robbed her of speech, but his anger cut her to the very core and the fragile blossom died as suddenly as it had been born.

How could he be here? She'd left him in Brisbane and . . . His anger! No wonder he was angry. She'd all but snubbed him on the telephone. What could she possibly expect from him? And for him to find her in Shann's arms . . .

'I'm free now, Devereaux.' Shann had recovered and even smiled down at Kezia. 'We were just having a little tête-à-tête, weren't we, Kez? About love.'

Her mouth was so dry with reaction that she couldn't have spoken if she'd tried, and she hadn't a skerrick of air in her lungs to even attempt it. It was all she could do to give a slight nod of her head as she felt the fire of a blush wash her cheeks.

A dark eyebrow rose ironically, although his blue eyes even icier. 'If you're ready,' he said impatiently.

'Sure. You're the boss, so to speak.' Shann took a step away from Kezia and stopped, turning back to give her a crooked smile. 'Maybe you should be the first to know. Meet the new owner of Cascade Court.'

Kezia's eyes flew to the man by the door in disbelief. Bligh Devereaux owned Cascade Court? The idea hadn't occurred to her. She had been so wrapped up in the fact that he was there at all to wonder what had brought him. Now it all fell into place—his visit to Norfolk Island, Shann's uncharacteristic deference, his presence at the auction sale. And now his return.

'Don't tell me you didn't even suspect, Kezia,' Shann teased, and she shook her head, her eyes on Bligh, who had turned partly away from them, impatience in the stiff line of his body. 'I feel I should warn you, Devereaux,' Shann walked to the door and stood waiting for Kezia to precede him out of the room, 'that Kezia McCoy is a veritable virago when it comes to Norfolk Island and guarding our birthright.' Although he was smiling there was an underlying edge to Shann's voice. 'So I suggest you check with her before you make any changes around here.'

Kezia wished the floor would open up and swallow her. How could Shann be so petty? He was only having a cheap jibe at her. She glanced up at him, her eyes resting on him with cool levelness, the Shann of her dreams so far apart from the reality that she could scarcely credit it. And he was the first to look away.

'I'll try to remember that,' Bligh remarked drily across her thoughts, and without another word he strode towards the reception area.

'Kez?' Shann began, but she walked away from him.

'Devereaux wants you, so I suggest you don't keep him waiting,' she retaliated as she almost ran back out to her taxi.

After that Kezia gave the Court a wide berth, even going so far as to ask Chris to take any taxi fare to or from there. Her brother's eyes were sympathetic and although he asked no questions she knew he thought Shann Evans was the reason for her restrained reluctance to go to the hotel.

Little did Chris know that she rarely thought about Shann. All her thoughts were of Bligh Devereaux, and although she tried to bar him from her mind, at an unguarded moment his face would appear, slipping beneath her armour, starting off the ache of loss once more.

That he was the new owner of the Court was something of a nine-day wonder, a topic colouring almost every conversation. And if he deliberately set out to charm the islanders he more than succeeded. They all thought he was a good bloke. Wherever she went Kezia's ear seemed to be supersensitively tuned to the sound of his name, and yet she never once heard mention of his wife. And short of actually coming straight out and asking someone, a thing she knew she would never be able to do without giving herself away, she would just have to patiently wait until the subject arose.

Busy taking the washing off the line, lost in a labyrinth of depressing thoughts, Kezia took a full couple of minutes to realise that the phone was ringing upstairs. Making a mad dash inside, she dropped her pile of sun-warmed sheets on a chair and grabbed for the receiver.

'Oh, Kez, I thought you were out,' her mother sounded a little flustered.

'Just out at the clothes line. What's wrong, Mum?' She sat down beside the phone, catching her breath.

'The taxi's broken down. I got a call from the airport and that rotten starter motor seems to be stuck again,' fumed her mother. 'Chris won't be back for at least an hour, so I wondered if you'd mind taking the mini-bus out to collect the two couples who've just arrived.'

'Sure, Mum. What are their names?'

'Benson and . . .' Allie shuffled some papers about, 'Here it is. Benson and Rivers. Kez, I'm sorry, but they're going to the Court,' she added quickly.

Kezia's fingers tightened on the receiver and she forced a lightness she didn't feel. 'That's all right. I'll go now.'

Allie sighed. 'Thanks, love. I'll see you later.'

It was highly unlikely that she would see Devereaux, Kezia told herself sternly. Look how busy Shann used to be. She stood up slowly and glanced down at her jeans and loose cheesecloth top. She should change, but . . . What the heck! Slipping her bare feet into a pair of sandals, she hurried out to the mini-bus.

When she reached the airport she spied her fare immediately. The two elderly couples were standing by their luggage looking lost, and she smiled at them and apologised for the breakdown, her open friend-liness putting them at ease and making them feel at home. She drove slowly through the shopping centre, pointing out various businesses and eating places. That she was in no hurry to get to Cascade Court had nothing to do with it, she told herself. Once there she would just drop off her holidaymakers and leave immediately.

With this decision firmly made she turned into the driveway, and then drew her breath in surprise. Old Sam Adams and a couple of young men she knew by sight were hard at work, tanned muscular backs bent under the hot sun. Already they had cleared the tropical undergrowth from the left-hand side of the driveway and were piling the branches and bushes together to be carted away.

Kezia drew the mini-bus to a halt, but before she had switched off the engine and climbed down from the cab a red-coated porter, a young man not known to Kezia, was there to take charge of the two elderly couples and their luggage, ushering them up the steps and into the foyer. Kezia stared after them, feeling an irrational anger.

That was new, this great rush of service. Previously Kezia always had to deliver new arrivals to the reception desk herself. It was an improvement on the service—but she banished the thought from her mind. She turned back in the direction of the garden and her lips tightened. So Bligh Devereaux was very busy with his new broom already! She strode across to old Sam Adams, who gave her a cheery grin as she approached.

'Hello there, young Kezia. How are you?' He wiped a work-worn hand across his damp brow.

'Fine, Mr Adams. What's all this in aid of?' she asked, waving her arm in the direction of the activity.

'New boss's orders. Clean out the rubbish and get back to lawns,' replied the old man.

'Rubbish? What rubbish? There was some lawn already and the tropical surroundings are part of the Court's charm. Didn't you tell him so?' Kezia frowned.

'Not me, Kezia. I'm for an easy life. The boss says do it and I do it. Keeps me out of trouble.' He grinned 'I'm getting too old for trouble.'

Kezia glanced around at the already radically changed garden and fumed.

'Now something tells me you're going to go looking for a bit of trouble yourself,' old Sam laughed outright. 'And Mr Devereaux, he's the one to give it to you. He's a man who knows what he wants, that one.'

'Oh, does he?' said Kezia softly, old Sam's words fanning the flame that grew inside her. 'Bye, Mr Adams,' she remembered to add as she turned on her heel and headed towards the hotel entrance, unaware that the old man leaned on the handle of his rake and grinned after her.

'May I help you?' asked the same young porter as Kezia entered the hotel and glanced levelly about the foyer.

'I'd like to see Mr Devereaux,' she said without preamble, ignoring the sudden fluttering of her heart at the thought of seeing him again.

The young man's eyes went over Kezia's slim figure, her semi-see-through blouse and tight faded jeans. 'I'm sorry, Mr Devereaux's busy at present. Would you like to leave a message with our receptionist?'

Slanting a glance at the young girl behind the desk, Kezia's chin rose. 'No, thank you. I'm sure Bligh will see me,' she stated, and marched towards the hallway to the office, her cheeks flushing just a little as she spoke his name, and she was almost across the foyer before the young man recovered himself.

'Look, Mr Devereaux has left strict instructions that he's not to be disturbed,' he said, catching up to her and trying to put himself between Kezia and the office.

'He'll see me,' Kezia told him firmly, not slowing her stride.

They were in the short hallway now, within a pace or two of the closed office door, and the young porter took hold of Kezia's arm.

'Hey, come on! Mr Devereaux doesn't want to see anyone.' His voice had an edge to it now. 'I'm afraid you can't go in there.'

At that moment Kezia noticed that Shann's name had already been removed from the office door, and her lips tightened. It sure hadn't taken Devereaux long! Shann hadn't even left the island. She raised her hand and, to the consternation of the porter, gave a decisive knock and opened the door.

Bligh was seated at the desk poring over a large pile of papers stacked in front of him. The light glistened on the expensive gold pen he held in his hand while the long fingers of his other hand gently rubbed his forehead.

'I thought I said no interruptions,' he said, not

bothering to look up, his pen moving swiftly over the page.

'I'm sorry, sir,' began the young man. 'I tried to tell the young lady, but she insisted on coming in,' he finished lamely.

The dark head rose then, vivid blue eyes flashing towards them, staying locked on Kezia as she stood momentarily faltering just inside the office. Slowly he put down his pen and sat back in his chair, his hand running through his hair.

'That's all right, Pete, you can go,' he said, not taking his eyes from Kezia.

The young man slid a curious look at the girl beside him and then silently left them. His master, Kezia thought scornfully, had spoken.

'What can I do for you, Kezia?' Bligh stood up, unconsciously flexing his shoulder muscles as he walked around the desk. He had shed his jacket and tie and his light body shirt strained across the solid contours of his chest.

Some of Kezia's aggression wavered a little as her eyes rose to meet his; over the soft material of his pale blue shirt showing the V of dark curling hair on his chest where he'd undone the top few buttons; over the strong tanned column of his throat and the firm clean-shaven chin; over his lips that hinted at a heart-stopping sensuousness she knew full well they possessed; up to meet his eyes, fringed by dark masculine lashes, eyes that same incredible blue of the clear clean seas on a bright sunshiney day. Somehow sitting down he wasn't quite so formidable, and she had to blink to make herself remember why she was there.

'I've just seen old Sam Adams working in the garden, and you're ruining the whole setting of the place!' she got out in a rush, her dark eyes flashing.

'I'd hardly call clearing up the garden ruining it.' He raised a dark eyebrow.

'Maybe you wouldn't, but that lush tropical foliage has always been part of the Court's charm.' Her hands went to her hips and she braced her feet slightly apart, unconsciously preparing for battle.

'There's a distinct difference between natural foliage and plain out-and-out neglect,' Bligh said evenly, leaning back against the desk and folding his arms, his body shirt moulding the firm muscles of his broad shoulders.

'Neglect! Shann hasn't neglected the Court,' she burst out. 'It's been his life and he's worked hard, as his father did before him.'

'I'm not saying he hasn't. But there are some facets of the place that I think need refurbishing.' He held up one hand as she went to interrupt. 'Kezia, the only undergrowth I'm clearing out is the cherry guava. From what I've heard it's starting to take over the vegetation of the island, so cutting it back from around the Court is not going to endanger its future by any means. I simply think that extended green lawns and flowering hibiscus would do more for the Court's appearance than untamed bush.'

'Just because you're taking over you feel you have to change everything!' Her face flushed angrily and perversely she refused to admit that what he said had more than a little truth. 'We don't want any carbon copies of the mainland. We like things to be natural, and you take it from me, we don't like outsiders coming over here and trying to change everything!'

'I'm not trying to change anything simply for the sake of it,' he said, pushing away from the desk and moving closer to her. 'I'm a businessman. Business is my livelihood and I'm not going to let this investment fall down about my ears in case I offend anyone by doing a few small jobs of maintenance and modernisation.'

'The Court is one of the best and most modern motels on the island, and Shann made it that,' she said defiantly, standing her ground, her eyes darkly bright with anger, refusing to let his calm matter-of-factness douse her anger.

'That's as may be,' he said quietly and his blue eyes coldly met hers. 'But I'm going to change Cascade Court from being one of the best to irrefutably *the* best motel on the island. And that's a promise, Kezia.' His voice was deeply sensual as he said her name, and she couldn't prevent the tremor of pleasure that washed over her at the sound.

But that pleasure spelled danger, danger that she might succumb to his attraction, attraction he had no right to allow between himself and anyone else, save his wife. Her eyes met his, her wrath rekindling.

'You have no justifiable reason to criticise Shann,' she began.

'Let Shann Evans fight his own battles. He's old enough. And I don't think he'd welcome you trying to do it for him.' Bligh's voice was still even, but his jaw was now tense and his eyes were the shade of the shadowed ocean.

'How would you know what Shann would or wouldn't welcome?' she goaded, aware she was playing with fire but unable to back away from the flame.

'I know he wants to hit the high spots, the bright lights, and he wants a woman who wants what he wants to tag along. A woman like Raewyn Bourke.'

Not an inexperienced little virgin, in other words, Kezia reminded herself, the humiliation of that remembered moment passing over her face, and she flinched at the denigrating pain.

Bligh's body tensed and he stepped forward his hands reaching out to her shoulders. At his touch Kezia's eyes flew to his face.

'Forget him, Kezia. He doesn't deserve your advocacy,' he ground out roughly.

'Take your hands off me!' Kezia stumbled backwards out of his hold. 'What right have you got to talk about deserving?' Her voice was tight and strained. 'You're just an outsider who wants to flash his money about, and you don't care about spoiling our island doing it!'

'Now you're being ridiculous, Kezia, and if you gave yourself time to cool off you'd realise it,' he said clippedly.

'And after the garden,' she continued as though he hadn't spoken, 'what other little amendments are you going to make? A helicopter pad on the roof? A casino in the restaurant with topless go-go dancers?'

His hands were clamped on her shoulders again and she had nowhere to go to escape them, for her back was against the closed office door.

'Kezia, whatever I decide to do with my motel, make no mistake, it will be my decision and mine alone. I won't be consulting you or anyone.'

'I never asked you to consult me!' she threw back at him, her anger almost choking her while his nearness set her heartbeats stumbling erratically. 'I've never asked you for anything.' The words were out before she could stop them and the pain she felt made her voice sound thin and tight.

'Haven't you?' he asked, his lips stiff and cold, his eyes, as frozen as the waves on a grey and stormy sea, boring down into hers. 'Well, as I see it, you're asking now, and I'm damn well ready to give it,' he told her, his fingers biting into the soft flesh of her arms as his lips came down to crush hers.

CHAPTER EIGHT

THE pressure of his mouth was punishing, bruising her softness as she fought to escape him. Her hands went to his waist, pulling ineffectively at the material of his shirt, pushing powerlessly at the rock-hardness of his muscular body that was tensed against hers. When her fingernails raked at him he used his weight to pin her body against the door as his hands left her shoulders to seize her fingers and move them easily behind her back, capturing them there, shifting her weight from the cool impersonal panelling of the door to the warm wall of his conquering body.

Her arms caught firmly behind her arched Kezia still closer to him, her body touching his with an intimacy that began a spiralling assault on her traitorous defences. The torturing timbre of his kisses began to change, the punishment a persuasion, and she was powerless to prevent her lips parting beneath his as tiny shafts of pleasure rose inside her, enveloping her in a firey cocoon of mindless desire. Her whole body wanted to moan his name, moulded itself impossibly closer to the rapturous wonder of his.

His hard fingers released her hands and slid beneath the loose folds of her blouse, playing over her back to send searing shivers over her skin. Her own hands now climbed the tanned muscular arms, the firm well-developed shoulders, to wind around his neck, her fingers moving in the crisp darkness of his hair.

Gentle now, his lips teased hers, surrendering her

143

mouth for the sensitiveness of her earlobe and a sigh of delight broke from her as she sought the ecstasy of his lips again. He shifted his stance and her back was against the door again while his hands trailed molten fire beneath her thin blouse sliding over the sensitised skin of her ribcage to cover her breasts. Kezia felt a curious lightness in her legs and heard her voice, so unlike her own, sigh his name.

With practised confidence his hands were arousing beyond endurance while the pressure of his thighs imprisoned her with passionate ease. Not that she was making any attempt to escape, all thought of flight had left her. Her body had now surrendered, yielded completely and unconditionally as a tiny voice from somewhere far away told her she was wavering on the brink of no return, that she was fast losing the ability and the inclination to draw a halt to their lovemaking.

Heedlessly her hand slid downwards to rest on his chest, the heavy thudding of his heartbeats washing a wave of weakness over her again, engulfing her, and she trembled in his arms. She heard him catch a ragged breath and his arms folded around her, holding her painfully close as his lips found the velvet hollow at the side of her throat.

'Kezia McCoy, this has to stop,' he moaned softly, the fanning of his breath, the sweet touch of his lips making her skin tingle, and she unconsciously wriggled closer to him.

He drew a deep breath then and put a little space, a cold yawning chasm, between them, his hands lightly spanning her waist. Her eyes went upwards to meet his, her tongue-tip moistening her lips, and his fingers tightened. 'Kezia,' he groaned so quietly she barely caught the sound.

But the shock of the unconcealed desire she saw in his eyes, on his face, in the tenseness of his entire body brought her down to earth with an almighty thud. What had she done? What had possessed her to behave so . . .? God, what must her think of her, all but throwing herself at him? She had allowed him to twist her anger into arousal, her repulsion into capitulation. She had invited him to make love to her, almost begged him not to stop. If he had laid her down on the carpet right here and now she doubted she would . . . her eyelids fell downwards in shame.

'Kezia?' His voice flowed softly over her like liquid silk, but she kept her eyes tightly closed. 'Look at me!' he said, a quiet command, and his finger lifted her chin.

Her eyes fluttered open and as they met his she felt a slow blush wash her cheeks. A crooked smile lifted the corners of his mouth and with a sigh he stepped away from her.

'Can't say much for our timing,' he said ruefully, and ran a hand around the back of his neck, making his shirt front strain open, showing his strong tanned chest with its cover of fine dark hair.

The flame in Kezia's eyes flared as her gaze flickered over him, re-igniting a wave of pure wanting that threatened to overcome her. Her fire matched his, and she had taken a step towards him and one of his hands had found the soft dark curls at the nape of her neck when there was a sharp rap on the door behind Kezia. Almost simultaneously the door swung open, catching Kezia in the small of her back and knocking her forward into Bligh's arms. They both turned towards the voice that spoke in surprise.

'Kezia!' Shann was full of concern. 'Sorry about that. I didn't know you were here. Did I hurt you?'

'No. No, of course not. Just startled me.' She pushed herself upright out of Bligh's arms, flushing at the sensations he could so easily create with his unconsciously arousing fingers. History was repeating itself, the scene was playing again. Kezia with Shann, enter Bligh. Kezia with Bligh, enter Shann. An hysterical giggle rose and she choked it off.

'Don't leave because of me,' Shann said quickly. 'I'll only keep you a minute.' He looked at Devereaux.

'No, that's all right. Goodbye,' Kezia tossed at them both, and all but ran from the office, her heartbeats hammering, refusing to settle even as she drove the mini-bus out on to the road. And she never gave the garden a glance as she left, feeling as though the devil himself was on her tail.

Unconsciously she turned down Rooty Hill Road and pulling the bus to a stop overlooking Emily Bay, her head fell slowly on to her hands as she leant on the steering wheel. Never had she felt so down.

In blind misery she sat wondering how she was going to go on facing Bligh after this. If he was looking for an easy affair—an extra-marital affair, she reminded herself harshly—then she had given him more encouragement, making herself so very readily available. There weren't enough adjectives to describe her foolishness, and it was some time before she started the mini-bus and turned it slowly homewards.

'I'll just slip up to the bakery, Kez,' said Allie McCoy, 'if you don't mind holding the fort here.'

'No, Mum, I'll be fine. I've got the rest of these accounts to do,' Kezia replied absently, not glancing up, missing the sharp look her mother gave her as her tiredness hung in the tone of her voice. To say she'd been sleeping badly lately was an understatement.

'All right. I won't be long.' Allie decided not to pass comment and turned to leave the office, pausing as a tall figure entered. 'Oh, hello there, Shann. What can we do for you?' Her eyes went momentarily to Kezia, who had glanced up quickly from her paperwork, her pale cheeks tinged with pink.

'Nothing, thanks, Allie.' Shann's smile charmed. 'Purely a social call. As I probably won't get time to call at your house I thought I'd say goodbye now while you're here and I'm passing.'

'You're leaving the island, then?' asked Allie quietly. 'We'll miss you, Shann.' She reached up and kissed him on the cheek.

'I'll miss you, too,' replied Shann sincerely, 'and your fantastic cooking.' He gave Allie a hug. 'I guess I ate at your house more often than I did at home when I was a kid.'

Allie laughed and then sobered. 'I hope all goes well for you, Shann.'

'Thanks, Allie.' Shann's eyes went to Kezia and Allie followed his gaze, a shadow of a frown on her forehead.

'Well, I was just off to the bakery. 'Bye, Shann, and good luck.' She patted his hand and was gone.

Shann turned slowly back towards Kezia and walked over to sit on the edge of her desk. 'How's things, Kez?' he asked softly.

'Fine,' she replied a little breathlessly, her cheeks flushing, knowing Shann was pretty well aware of just what he had interrupted in Bligh's office a few days ago. 'When . . . When will you actually be leaving?'

'A couple of days' time.' He shrugged. 'Funny, I've

been looking forward to going for so long and now that it's almost time to go I'm getting this urge to want to stay.' He gave a rather forced laugh. 'Maybe my roots here have gone deeper than I thought.'

Kezia looked up at him, wondering if he spoke the truth or if he was offering a part apology for his harsh comments on their heritage.

'I guess we can't turn back the clock, though,' he sighed, picking up a shiney glass paperweight and moving it in his hand.

'Can you stop the sale of the motel?' she asked him. Perhaps it wasn't too late for Bligh . . .

'No.' Shann shook his head. 'That's well and truly through. Devereaux doesn't let the grass grow under his feet, that's for sure.' His voice held a hint of irony as his gaze moved over Kezia's slim figure in her neat uniform, giving his words an unsubtle double meaning.

'Well, I guess what's done is done,' said Kezia quickly. 'Where will you be going from here?'

'Sydney for a start, then on to London.' His eyes continued to watch her and she shifted uncomfortably.

'That should be nice.' She wished she could control her rising colour. Shann had never looked at her quite so boldly, and she realised she didn't like it any more than she liked his kisses.

'Yes. Nice,' he repeated flatly, and smiled without much humour. 'I'm going on something of a Grand Tour of the Continent, wherever the fancy takes me.' He paused, his eyes dropping to the rise and fall of her breasts beneath her sedate orange uniform. 'I'd rather fancy taking you with me, Kez,' he added softly, replacing the paperweight on the desk, his fingers going out to cover hers.

'Shann, please!' Kezia tried to draw her hand away. 'That's impossible, you know that.'

'Do I? I thought you liked me?' His hold tightened on her wrist and he bent his head to kiss the back of her hand.

'I do like you, Shann, but,' Kezia swallowed, 'my . . . my life's here on the island. I don't want to leave.'

'Don't you want to see a little of the world?' Shann persisted.

'No, not at present. I like it here.' She tried again to pull her hand away from his hold. 'Please, let me go, Shann.'

He slowly released her. 'We could have a great time together, Kez.'

'I thought Raewyn would be going with you,' Kezia said evenly, and a frown touched Shann's brow and was as quickly gone.

'Perhaps.' He shrugged and Kezia raised an eyebrow in surprise. 'She's visiting friends in New Zealand. We may run into each other in London.'

His eyes didn't quite meet Kezia's and she suspected that he wasn't being strictly truthful. But what possible reason could he have for pretending a break with Raewyn? Unless they had had an argument.

'You know, I can't see what this place holds for you, Kez.' Shann motioned to the tourist office. 'I mean, what's so great about it all?'

'It's my home,' she said simply, 'and I enjoy my job and my life style. And I enjoy meeting people.'

'I see. I wonder,' he caught his bottom lip between his teeth reflectively, 'would you have come with me if I'd asked you, say, six months ago?'

Six months ago. Before Bligh Devereaux. She

glanced up at him and then quickly away. Six months ago she had been all wrapped up in her fantasy of love and marriage, her adolescent dreams, a joining of the Evans and the McCoys. Right, somehow, a continuance of the past.

But the real world didn't quite work that way. It wasn't as rosy or as black and white. She'd had all the colours wrong. And love, the love she wanted to share for life, wasn't the crystal-clear fairytale she had thought it was. It was so very much more, a whole new variegation of pleasure and pain, of wonder and hurting . . . And it should have been a gift of giving and the joy of receiving.

'Well, Kezia?' Shann's voice drew her back to the present, and the pain crept about her heart and brought a rush of tears to her eyes. She had given her heart to Bligh Devereaux and he had taken it, knowing full well he had no right to do so.

'Kezia?' Shann strode around the desk to take her in his arms. 'Hey, Kezia, don't cry! Look, I was only teasing you—you know me. I didn't mean to hurt your feelings. I was trying to get to you for not jumping at the chance to head off with me.' He grimaced self-derisively. 'Call it my bruised ego. And you, of all people, don't deserve to suffer for that.' His fingers tightened on her shoulder as he gave her a hug. 'I'm a selfish bastard, aren't I?'

'It wasn't you, Shann, really. I guess I'm just tired. I didn't sleep very well last night.' Kezia dashed the dampness from her cheeks with the back of her hand and looked up to meet Shann's eyes, to find him watching her sharply.

'It's him, isn't it?' he asked quietly.

'Who?' Kezia's voice wavered thinly.

'Devereaux. Bligh Devereaux.' There was an edge of bitterness in Shann's tone. 'I suspected it from the beginning, but I wasn't sure until I interrupted you in the office the other day.'

'Shann!' Kezia broke in on him. 'I barely know Bligh Devereaux.' She forced a laugh. 'You're imagining things.'

'Am I? I don't think so somehow. I think you're stuck on the guy.'

Kezia's eyes fell from his.

'So what's the trouble, then?' Shann asked. 'It can't be that he doesn't feel the same way about you. From the first moment he saw you he's had trouble dragging his eyes away from you. And in the office, when I walked in on you, if looks could have killed he'd have put me out of my misery. As I see it all that's left is for me to ask you to name your first boy after me,' he smiled, if a little stiffly.

'Oh, Shann!' Kezia turned her face into the softness of his shirt, the now familiar pain clutching at her heart. 'Everything's wrong.'

'Wrong? You love him, don't you?' he asked, and Kezia nodded. 'So why?'

'Because he's already married,' she told him flatly.

'Married? Devereaux? Kez, are you sure?' Shann held her away from him so that he could look straight at her. 'It's the first I've heard of any marriage.'

'I saw his wife in Brisbane,' she said, a catch in her voice. 'She's . . . she's very attractive.'

'Then where is she, his wife? I mean, she's not on the island, that's for sure, and as he intends living here why isn't she with him? Are they divorced or something?'

'I don't know. Maybe she'll be joining him once he

gets settled in,' Kezia grimaced. 'I did see her with my own eyes, Shann.'

Shann seemed at a loss for words. 'He never once gave me the impression he was married. Not that he spoke much about his family, only once a little about his father. God, he's got a nerve!' he finished angrily. 'And to think I actually asked you to be nice to him! I can tell you, Kez, I'm not very proud of that. But,' he lifted his shoulders, 'I wanted to sell the Court and he had the cash. I can't say I've ever really liked him much, though.'

'You didn't ask me to fall for him,' Kezia said softly. 'I managed that piece of foolishness all by myself.'

'Kez, come with me,' said Shann after a pause. 'To Sydney—to London. You could do with a break, a new scene, new people. I could look after you.'

Kezia smiled a little cynically. 'And Raewyn would understand?'

Shann's dark eyes flickered before he spoke. 'Sure she would.'

'I can't see it, Shann, and neither can you. I wouldn't in her place. It wouldn't be fair of you to ask her. Besides,' Kezia gave a soft bitter laugh, 'the problem's the same, it's there no matter where I take it.'

Shann strode a few paces around the desk before turning back to face her. 'What will you do?'

'Nothing.' She shrugged. 'Stay here. Keep on doing what I'm doing.'

'You mean you'll stay here and face him! Every day?' Shann asked in surprise tinged with exasperation.

'It is my home. I lived here before he came and I'll go on living here regardless. I probably won't see him very often anyway,' she finished with more conviction in her voice than she had in her heart. Just talking about him set her heart aching, but she doggedly told herself the pain would pass.

Shann's face was all sympathy. 'You've got guts. I'm sorry it didn't work out, Kez.'

'I'll get over it.' She stood up and walked with him to the door, his arm draped compassionately about her shoulders.

'You're coming to the party tomorrow night, aren't you?' he asked, turning to face her as they stood in the wide sliding glass doorway.

'Your farewell party?' She nodded. 'Chris assures me I'm going with him and his latest girl-friend, what's-her-name? Suzie, the Aussie girl who works at the Hillcrest.'

'Good. I'll see you tomorrow night, then.' His hands cupped her cheeks. 'You'll always be special to me, Kez,' he said, and kissed the tip of her nose before striding away up the footpath.

Kezia leant back against the door jamb and sighed. Shann would always be special to her, too—not as the love of her life but as the hero of her youth. She smiled wryly to herself. Even if Shann didn't possess the gallant and noble qualities with which she had endowed him.

Her eyes followed Shann's figure as he turned and lifted his hand before he climbed into his car. She smiled and returned his wave. His departure from the island would take the last threads of her adolescence with him, for she knew she had done a lot of growing up, emotional growing up, since Bligh Devereaux had made his appearance in their lives.

As Shann's car disappeared along the street her gaze

slid pensively along the opposite footpath, only to
freeze on the figure standing by the bank, his own eyes
fixed on her. Her heartbeats did a back somersault in
her breast and her breath caught somewhere between
her lungs and her lips.

Bligh's whole stance was tension and aggression,
and even from this distance she could see the
unsmiling line of his lips, the harsh set of his jaw,
could feel the disapproval, the displeasure emanating
from him. Obviously, he must have been watching her
and Shann and clearly he didn't like what he'd seen.
How dared he!

Pushing herself away from the support of the door
jamb, Kezia turned defiantly to face him. He had no
right to criticise her or Shann. The vivid blueness of
his eyes held hers with lazer sharpness for what
seemed like an eternity before they travelled over her
body in lazy insolence. Then he continued on into the
bank.

Slowly Kezia set free the breath that had been
captured inside her and returned to her desk, her body
burning where his eyes had touched her. He had no
right, she repeated to herself. He had no right to
judge, to condemn, and he had no right to look at her
the way he had.

Her head sank to rest on the hand she wiped shakily
across her burning eyes. Bligh had no right to look at
her like that, no right to touch her, no right to . . . A
hot teardrop made a glistening trail down her flushed
cheek.

'Chris has told me all about you, Kezia,' smiled the
little blonde girl sitting at the table opposite Kezia.

'All bad, I'll bet,' Kezia grimaced at her brother
who, she had to admit, looked very handsome in his

light safari suit. She had been pleasantly surprised to find she really liked Chris' girl-friend, Suzie, a petite twenty-year-old who appeared to be all big eyes behind large-framed glasses, and long silky fair hair.

'Not all, Sis,' Chris laughed, and put his arm along the back of Suzie's chair. 'In fact, I actually admitted that you're a real treasure, one we couldn't do without.'

Kezia groaned in mock disbelief and shook her head, refusing to rise to Chris's bait.

'Hi! How about a drink with the guest of honour?' Shann asked, laughing as he joined them. 'Enjoying yourselves?' He refilled their glasses from the bottle of champagne he'd brought with him.

'To good luck and your good time.' Chris raised his glass and they drank a toast.

'Come on, Kez, it's a pity to waste the band. Dance with me? With big brother's permission, of course,' Shann grinned teasingly at Chris.

Chris shot a quick assessing look at Kezia and she smiled easily at him. 'I think I can trust you not to spirit me away, Shann, and besides, I choose my own partners. I'm a big girl now, haven't I told you already?'

'I won't deny that,' Shann beamed at her, and took her hand. 'Excuse us.'

Shann swung her on to the floor. 'You look divine tonight,' he whispered in her ear, his hands drawing her closer.

'And you are ever so slightly tipsy, Shann Evans.' She put one hand against his chest to keep some space between them.

'Are you suggesting, Miss McCoy, that I'm drunk? At my own farewell party? I'm wounded, Kez, mortally wounded. I've never been soberer in my life,' he lisped exaggeratedly.

'Well, shall we say very happy?' Kezia giggled softly, beginning to relax.

'Ah, that's more like it. Now I feel like I'm holding something soft and cuddly in my arms and not something stiff and starched. What's the matter, love? Aren't you having a good time?' he asked sympathetically.

'Nothing's the matter, and yes, I'm having a good time,' Kezia told him. At least she was enjoying herself as much as she possibly could wondering if Bligh would turn up any minute.

The party was being held in one of the smaller function rooms at Cascade Court and although she rather doubted that Shann would invite Devereaux it was on the cards that he could put in an appearance. When she'd just arrived with Chris and Suzie she'd been as taut as a bowstring, filled with a nerve rending mixture of anticipation and apprehension, but as the evening wore on and the later it got the more unlikely it seemed that he would join the party. Whether she was gratified or disappointed she refused to analyse.

'Great! I want you to have a good time,' Shann was saying. 'You know, it's not considered good manners to be melancholy at someone's farewell party.' Shann smiled teasingly at her and then spun her around to the music.

'Shann, stop! You're making me dizzy!' Kezia laughed, and clutched at his arms to steady herself as he slowed them down to a halt. Kezia stayed leaning up against him as they laughed together.

'Ah, Kez, I'm really going to miss you,' Shann said softly, his eyes dark and luminous.

'Until you get so taken up with all the new sights, the new people you'll meet,' she said lightly, sensing the stillness in him as his arms tightened around her. 'You'll have to write and tell me all about it.'

'I'd much rather show you.' His voice was low and suggestively liquid, his lips resting against her temple. 'Mmm! I've got this fantastic idea. Let's slip outside for some fresh air,' he murmured persuasively. 'It's getting very stuffy in here.'

Kezia pushed gently against his chest, her dark eyes smiling as she looked up at him. 'What? Leave your own party? Now that is considered gross bad manners.'

'Who'll miss us?' he persisted, dancing them in the direction of the doorway.

'Chris and Suzie for starters,' Kezia told him, keeping her voice even as she searched the dancers surreptitiously for her brother.

'Three's a crowd, Kez. If I know Chris he'll be all attentive to Suzie. And we surely don't need an audience. We won't even need the band,' he chuckled. 'I swear no one will even notice that we've gone.'

'I don't want to leave the party, Shann,' Kezia said softly and firmly.

'Don't tell me a big girl like you is scared to be alone with harmless old me?' he teased, his hand moving over the small of her back.

They were almost to the edge of the dance floor now and Kezia felt a rising impotent anger. Damn men and their oh-so-sure-of-themselves conceited attitudes! She'd had her fill of it.

'Shann, if you don't stop this right now I'll make a scene. I wasn't joking when I said I didn't want to go outside.'

Shann looked down at her with a laugh, but at her expression the smile faded to be replaced by a frown of annoyance. 'You really mean it, don't you?' he said in surprise.

She nodded. 'Now, do we dance or do I go back and sit down?'

He shrugged sulkily. 'You don't have to get all uptight, Kez. But at least I'm not married and looking for a bit of fun on the side!'

Kezia stiffened away from him and felt the blood leave her face.

'God, I'm sorry, Kez!' Shann's arms tightened around her and he was all contrite. 'You're right, I must be drunk.' He smiled ruefully, his face touched with his old charm. 'Say you'll forgive me?' he asked winningly.

'I think I'd like to sit down now, Shann,' Kezia said softly, amazed again that she could have not seen the selfish immaturity in him.

'Ah, Kez, come on! I said I was sorry. I guess I'm just getting all upset about leaving and all that.' He moved his cheek against her hair.

'All right, Shann. But I would like to go back to the table.'

He sighed exasperatedly. 'I wonder if you know what you're missing, Kezia?' There was an edge to his teasing tone.

'That's my business.' Her eyes fell from his as her memory threw up those same words: inexperienced little virgin.

Biting off a not too polite exclamation, Shann pulled her not very gently back into his arms. 'You know, at this moment I could almost wish you on friend Devereaux.'

Even as the pain lanced through her Kezia's hand was lifted from Shann's arm and a deep mocking voice sliced between them like a wedge.

'The good fairy sends her regards, Evans. Your wish has been granted.'

CHAPTER NINE

SHAME washed over Kezia as Bligh swung her expertly into the group of dancers, not waiting for any comment from Shann. What could he be thinking Shann meant by his last remark? Her eyes slid back towards the door in time to see Shann taking an offered glass of beer from someone and downing it in one gulp. Judging by the amount of alcohol he'd already consumed the beer was not going to improve his disposition. Shann's gaze found Kezia and Bligh and Kezia saw the anger blaze in his expression before he turned and pulled another girl to her feet and joined the dancers. If she could get to Chris maybe he could restrain Shann a little.

Her eyes went back to her hand where it rested on Bligh's shoulder, her focus unconsciously registering the fine weave of his expensive suit jacket, and thoughts of Shann faded completely from her mind. Bligh's hand on her back and his fingers clasping hers were sending bittersweet tremors of delight through her body and she stiffened, not wanting him to feel her awareness of him.

And she was aware of him, with every fibre of her being. Now her eyes slid to his tie, were drawn irresistibly upwards over his cream collar to the tanned column of his throat, and she closed her eyes, fighting the almost overwhelming urge to put her lips against the smooth texture of his skin, torturing herself with the realisation that the journey over his chin to the apogee of his lips was so tormentingly short.

'I take it that Evans' wish is not yours?' The sound of his voice startled her into looking up to meet his gaze. His face had a tensed, closed look about it and the blueness of his eyes was hidden beneath his lowered eyelids. But somehow she knew they moved over her, taking in the soft moulding material of her leisure suit, its pastel lemon shade and cream unbleached calico collar and trim complementing her olive skin and dark hair.

'Wish?' she stammered, her brain sluggishly refusing to compute the word.

His lips thinned and then he shrugged cynically. 'No matter. We'll leave it for now.'

He continued to dance, holding her lightly in his arms, but Kezia's legs felt heavy and the tension between them intensified until she thought it could only explode about them.

'I . . . I didn't know you would be coming to the party,' she ventured at last, unable to endure the quietness a moment longer. For all the noise being made by the musicians and the party-makers combined, the silence between herself and Bligh clamoured in her ears.

'I'd just arrived,' he replied, and expertly guided her out of the path of an over-energetic couple. 'Evans gave me a token invitation. It would have been impolite to refuse.' His tone gave his words the completely opposite meaning.

'I'm sure Shann is pleased you could come,' Kezia said, embarrassed, and flushed at the inanity of her remark.

'Are you, Kezia?' he asked quietly. 'I'd say when I

arrived on the scene Evans would have cheerfully liked to throw me out.'

Kezia swallowed nervously.

'He didn't somehow give me the impression that he wanted you rescued at that particular moment,' Bligh continued evenly.

'I don't know what gave you that idea.' Kezia made an attempt at a laugh. 'We were just dancing.'

'Your face called for rescue. I could see you looking for your brother. He's over at the bar talking to a group of people, by the way. As he was occupied, I stepped in.' He paused and glanced down at her. 'It was the least I could do. Aren't you going to thank me?' he asked drily.

Kezia pulled herself together. 'Yes, of course. Thank you. But there was really no need.'

'Evans was under the weather. I don't think he'd have been that easy for you to handle if he became belligerent.'

'I've known Shann all my life. He wouldn't harm me,' Kezia denied hotly.

'Wouldn't he?'

'No. He respects me.' She had a fleeting recollection of Shann pulling her ungently into his arms and a shadow passed over her face.

Bligh bit off something imprecatory. 'He wasn't taking you outside, away from the crowd?'

At Kezia's blush he smiled humourlessly.

'He . . . If you must know, he . . . he asked me to go with him tomorrow, to Sydney,' she threw at him, some of her bottled-up hurt escaping to goad her, and she felt his whole body tense, like a coiled spring, a jungle cat ready to pounce.

'And are you going?' he asked at last, when she

thought he had had enough of the subject, was prepared to drop it there.

'Probably,' she stretched the truth defensively.

'What about Raewyn Bourke? Where does she fit into this?' His eyes stabbed her with controlled angry barbs and Kezia shrugged indifferently, not able to find an answer.

'Don't you mind sharing him?' he demanded burtally.

'What makes you think I'll be sharing?' Kezia got out with no little effort.

'Because he was speaking to her on the phone in my office this evening and they didn't sound,' he paused, 'estranged.'

Kezia's eyes fell from his, her defiance dying, and she swallowed nervously, wishing she hadn't instigated this particular trend in the conversation.

'Well, Kezia, do you mind sharing? It could be very cosy, the three of you.'

His words made her go cold inside and the need to hit back at him seized her again.

'You can talk! What gives you the right to judge?' she blazed at him lowering her voice as several heads turned in their direction.

'I'm not judging him, Kezia. I'm trying to open your eyes, wake you up to Shann Evans. Why throw yourself away on a man who doesn't know what the word "faithful" means?'

Anger stabbed in Kezia's chest as Dale Devereaux's face swam before her eyes. God, he had a nerve! How could he be so hypocritical? Her hand itched to slap the controlled expression from his face. She dragged a calming breath and stepped back from him.

'I'm going to sit down,' she said with as much

composure as she could muster, and turned back towards their table.

When she reached out for her chair Bligh's hand was there before hers and to her chagrin he sat himself down beside her.

'I'd appreciate being by myself,' she told him through clenched teeth, wanting him to go and stay at the same time, her eyes searching again for Chris. He was by the bar, standing with his back to her, but Suzie caught her eye and casually touched Chris's arm and extricated them from the group of young people standing with them.

As Chris and Suzie joined them Bligh stood up.

'Hi!' smiled Chris easily, not noticing Kezia's stiff withdrawal.

'You must be Chris,' Bligh smiled back. 'I see the family resemblance. I'm Bligh Devereaux.' He extended his hand.

'Don't know how we haven't met before.' Chris shook the other man's hand. 'But I've sure heard a lot about you from Kezia and just about everyone else on the island.' He grinned. 'Oh, and this is Suzie James.'

Bligh smiled at Suzie and Kezia could see that the girl was impressed. Well, she was welcome to him, the . . .

'You've got a good piece of property in the Court,' Chris's words interrupted her irritated train of thought as he sat down at the table. 'We—the family, that is—only wish we could have raised the money to buy it.'

'Yes. It was an opportunity that doesn't crop up every day,' Bligh agreed drily.

'Will you be running the show yourself or putting in a manager?' Chris asked him.

'I'll be staying.' His eyes went to Kezia with a half shuttered look that made her feel cold and hot all over. 'I intend to run the motel myself.'

'Great! We have a fantastic way of life here on the island, but knowing Kezia I suppose she's told you that already. She's not a tour guide for nothing, are you, Sis?' he laughed. 'What happened to Shann, by the way?' Chris asked when neither Kezia nor Bligh appeared to want to comment.

'He's dancing with a dark-haired girl over there,' answered Suzie. 'He doesn't look too steady on his feet.'

Chris glanced across the dancers and frowned. 'I think he'd had a few before the party. Maybe he feels a bit upset about leaving now that the day draws near. I guess I'd better keep an eye on him. He'll have a king-size hangover tomorrow.'

'Shann's old enough to look after himself, I would have thought,' stated Suzie blandly. 'And speaking of Shann, here he comes.'

'Well, well, a gathering of the clan!' Shann all but fell into a chair. 'Do I see empty glasses? Here you are, Kezia, my love. A sip of champers will loosen you up.'

Beside her Kezia felt Bligh stiffen and she made no attempt to touch the glass that Shann pushed unsteadily towards her.

'No, thank you, Shann,' she kept her voice light. 'I was about to call it a night.' She looked pointedly at Chris.

'I'll take you home, love,' Shann said immediately. 'No need to bother Chris and Suzie.'

'I'll be taking Kezia home.' Bligh stood up, putting his hand with light restraint on Shann's shoulder.

'Don't get up, Evans. You can't be leaving your own party.' He took Kezia's arm and drew her to her feet.

'Hey, I said I'd take Kezia home,' Shann frowned, and struggled to stand, with only Chris's quick reflexes saving his chair from clattering backwards on to the floor.

'Don't worry, Shann,' Kezia put in quickly, knowing Shann was incapable of driving in his present state. 'Stay and enjoy your party. I'll see you tomorrow at the airport.'

'Let's go talk to the guys at the bar, mate,' Chris hastily distracted the other man and lead him away from the table, waving to Kezia behind Shann's back and motioning Suzie to follow him.

'I can ring my mother to come and pick me up,' Kezia said firmly as she walked with Bligh towards the foyer, his hand on her disturbingly firm, seeming to dare her to attempt to break away from him.

'Why bother your mother? I told Chris I'd see you home,' he remarked uncompromisingly as Kezia paused by the reception desk. His pressure on her arm had them across the carpet and he was opening the swinging doors, following her down the steps and motioning her towards a largish four-door sedan, one of their own more luxurious hire cars. He waited until she was seated inside, closed the door and strode around to the driver's side.

'I didn't know you'd hired one of our cars,' she said as he reached for the ignition, searching for words to fill the quietness, afraid of another tension charged silence.

'I picked it up yesterday. Allie has kindly let me have it until my own car arrives on the next ship.' He drove down to the roadway and turned in the opposite direction to Kezia's house.

'You should have turned right. We're going the wrong way,' she told him quickly.

'I know. I want to talk to you,' he said without expression, his hands moving easily on the steering wheel and gear lever.

Kezia's mouth opened, but it was a few moments before she'd recovered to speak. 'I don't see that we have anything to discuss so I'd appreciate it if you'd turn around and take me home.'

'Not until we talk,' he said with infuriating calmness.

'Look, I'm tired and I just want to go home,' Kezia enunciated slowly and clearly, but received no response. 'If you don't stop the car I'll jump out!' Her fingers felt for the door handle.

'Don't be silly, Kezia.' He turned the car down Rooty Hill Road. 'I simply want to talk to you and I'd prefer it that we didn't have an audience. Surely that's not asking too much?'

'It depends on what you want to talk about?' Kezia said warily. A little voice from somewhere round her heart was telling her to enjoy this added bonus of time spent with him, knowing his hard body was only a hand's touch away, while her head told her not to be foolish, to remember he wasn't to be trusted.

Bligh didn't enlighten her, not speaking until he had pulled the car off the road in the exact spot where she had stopped Shann's Alfa the afternoon she had driven him to the beach. The moon was almost full and lit the water enough to distinguish Philip and Nepean Islands and highlight the white foam of the ocean breaking on the reefs. The wind whistled around the car and the rustle of nearby leaves and branches mingled with other sounds of the night.

'Have you told your family you're leaving with Evans?' Bligh came straight to the point as he leant back in his seat, one hand across the steering wheel, the other resting on his knee, so close and yet so far away from Kezia's own leg.

'No.' She looked down at her hands clasped in her lap.

'Aren't you leaving that sort of news rather late?'

'They'll know soon enough.' How she wished she could simply tell him the truth, admit she wouldn't be going anywhere, that she had no wish to go with anyone. Except him. And that was out of the question.

A shiver ran over her arm to warm the sudden coldness. She really should have brought a jacket as the thin terry-towelling short-sleeved leisure suit was no protection from the wind or the chill in her heart!

'You know, I can't help but feel that all this is out of character with you, Kezia.' His voice made her mind jump back to the present. 'And I wonder why?'

'If you mean you thought I was an inexperienced ... that I was a boring little adolescent from some isolated backwater then you were wrong,' she began angrily, the wound still close to the surface.

'Was I, Kez?' He caressed her with his tone. 'Was I so wrong in thinking that the life Shann Evans has to offer is not for you? Can you face living out of a suitcase, going from one jetsetting party to another, drinking, gambling, sleeping with whoever takes your eye on that particular night?'

Kezia shrank back against the seat. 'Shann won't ... He's not going to be like that. He just wants to travel, to see the world.'

'He's out for what he calls a good time.' Bligh voice

suddenly had an edge to it. 'And that's all you'd be to him, too. A good time.'

'That's not true!' she cried defensively. But was she defending Shann or herself? In a flash of clarity Kezia saw the truth in what Bligh so callously said. Shann did see her in the way that he implied and the realisation made her want to lash out at him for a mixture of confusing emotions. For his apparent indifference. For showing her another flaw in Shann's character.

'You know it is,' he said flatly.

'And you're so quick to point out faults in everyone else. What makes you think you're so perfect?' Her anger made her voice sound shrill in her ears.

'I thought we were talking about you and Shann Evans,' he reminded her.

'You were. I was talking about you. You sit and criticise everyone else, but you're not so lily-white.' Tears choked her throat, but she fought them back.

'I haven't professed to be,' he began angrily, then sighed exasperatedly, running his hand through his hair. 'All I'm asking is that you think again about going with Evans. And the consequences.'

'I have thought about it,' Kezia said defiantly.

'And have you thought how your mother will take your leaving?'

Kezia gave a harsh laugh. 'Good grief, now you're going to try to make me go all family-conscious! My mother would be the last person to stand in the way of anything I wanted to do. And for your information, how I feel about my family is my business, not yours.'

'Listen, you selfish little bitch!' His hands reached out and swung her cruelly around in the seat, his fingers biting into her shoulders.

'Don't you call me a bitch!' Kezia flamed at him, her fingers clawing at his where they gripped her painfully. 'And take your hands off me!'

'Take them off you? I should put you over my knee and whale the living daylights out of you.' He swore as her fingernail raked his wrist. 'But I'm beginning to wonder if you're bloody well worth it!' His anger reached out and burned her.

Kezia twisted frantically to be free of him, but somehow she was against the solid wall of his chest and the steel bands of his arms had locked her to him, her hands on his thin shirt transmitting the tantalising sensations of the accelerating thud of his heartbeats.

She should be pushing him away, twisting her head aside from the descent of his lips, using all her strength to fight him off ... But her hands were moving with a mind of their own, unfastening the buttons on his shirt, stealing inside to slide over the smoothness of his skin. Her body was abandoning her, moulding itself to the feverish hardness of his. And her lips were searching, had found his, were opening beneath the desperate demands of his strive for possession.

His kisses, long and drugging, were everything to her, water where she had gone thirsty, food where she had hungered, warmth where there had only been a lonely coldness. And the warmth became a fire raging through them both, consuming them, fusing them together in an embrace they were powerless to break.

His lips touched her forehead, her eyelids, her nose, the curve of her cheek, and her mouth slid along his jawline, over the slight beard roughness, to nibble his earlobe until he groaned her name and drew her fiercely, impossibly closer. His hands fanned the flame of her desire, slipping beneath the elasticised waistband of her suit top, to stimulate the skin of her midriff, to mould the mounds of her breasts that strained towards him.

'Dear God, Kezia, I want you!' he moaned raggedly, his lips returning to capture hers. 'Don't go with Evans,' he murmured torturedly against her mouth. 'I'd go insane at the thought of another man touching you like this. I want you for myself—all to myself.'

'I want you. I want you!' His words struck ice cold through her body, dousing the fires with cruel ease, and she stiffened, her hands now finding the strength to push away from him. Caught momentarily unaware, he let her go, only to reach out for her again.

'No! Don't touch me!' Her voice broke out of her and echoed in the confines of the car. 'Don't touch me. I can't bear it!' Her voice rose almost hysterically.

'Kezia, what the hell are you talking about?' His hands caught her arms, went to draw her close again, but she cringed further along the seat, slapping his hands away. 'Kezia!'

'Take me home. I . . . Don't ever touch me again. You . . . you revolt me!' The words chilled her as she heard them fall from her mouth, knowing they constituted the biggest lie she had ever told in her life. If she were honest she would have admitted that she revolted herself.

At her words she felt him stiffen and the silence between them screamed, making the air in the car heavy with tension.

'You weren't exactly giving that impression a few minutes ago,' he said with ominous quietness.

'I just want to go home.' She fumbled for the door

handle again. 'I'll walk,' she stammered agitatedly, her teeth beginning to chatter with reaction.

Bligh reached across her with one fluid movement, his body pressing momentarily, agonisingly, against her, and the lock clicked loudly. 'I said I'd drive you home and I will, so help me!'

Kezia could hear the restraint in his words, feel the tautness under such a fragile leash.

'Kezia . . .?' His deep voice appealed to her again and she shrank back, knowing how easily she could succumb, how frail were her own defences.

Bligh swore thoroughly under his breath. 'Okay! I get the message loud and clear.' He slid back behind the wheel and the engine roared to life. 'But a word of warning, Kezia,' he ground out. 'Next time you decide to lead a man on you'd better learn when to call enough, because, believe, me, you just about left it too late!'

He drove her home then, and his cold constraint was all about them, in the unhurried methodic way he drove, in the precise movements of his hands on the steering wheel, and in the air between them that grew so thick you could have cut it with a knife. When he drew to a halt in front of her house he reached across her to unlock the door and push it open, not touching her this time.

Stiffly Kezia climbed out and turned back to close the door, her throat and eyes aching with unshed tears. But that was purely a physical thing, and could in no way match the pain in her heart as his parting words reverberated inside her as she sought the safety of her room.

'Bon voyage, Miss McCoy!'

CHAPTER TEN

KEZIA led the middle-aged spinsters out to the taxi, settling them inside with a smile before depositing their suitcases in the boot. Apologising for the slight delay, she told them she had one package to collect from cargo and then she would have them safely deposited at their hotel on the edge of the shopping centre.

It was two days since Shann's disastrous farewell party, and still the excruciating hurt hadn't eased. With brutal vivid recall her mind kept replaying those moments she'd spent in Bligh's arms, and she could feel her muscles ache with the tightness that had gripped her ever since he had brought her home.

Still she was unable to believe she had actually allowed him to make love to her, and more incredible yet was the way her own body, her own lips, and her hands had matched his in their inciting demands. She was sick inside herself, her emotions swinging like an insane pendulum from shrinking guilt to sensual arousal.

She had gone with Chris to say goodbye to a very apologetic and hung-over Shann and knew only a release that he had left. Shann had been unable to meet her eyes until, slightly irritated with him, she had kissed him chastely on the cheek and wished him good luck. Chris had looked at her in mild surprise, a crooked smile lifting one corner of his mouth as he realised she had well and truly got over her infatuation for Shann, and they had both watched the small plane climb into the clear blue sky with undisguised relief.

'One parcel for the McCoys,' said the young man emerging from the cargo section and handing Kezia a small roped box. She thanked him, signing his receipt book, and was turning to walk away when a soft familiar voice halted her in her tracks.

'Excuse me, I was told you have a taxi for hire.'

Kezia's wide gaze met the young woman's in horror as she froze to the spot.

'I've seen you somewhere before, haven't I?' Dale Devereaux frowned in concentration before her pretty face broke into a beaming smile. 'Of course! At the auction sale in Brisbane. You were talking to Bligh, weren't you?'

A multitude of excruciatingly uncomfortable feelings tumbled over each other inside Kezia—guilt, anger, betrayal, remorse. But the other girl was watching her, her eyes clear and untroubled, waiting for Kezia to confirm or deny.

'Yes.' Kezia swallowed and tried her voice again. 'Yes, I was at the auction.'

'I knew I'd seen you. Bligh would have introduced us if you hadn't had to rush off. I'm Dale Devereaux. How do you do?' She held out her hand and Kezia slowly took it. 'Kezia, isn't it?'

'Kezia McCoy,' she managed to reply, almost speechless with surprise.

'So we meet at last, Kezia. Such a pretty name!' Dale Devereaux's smile widened. 'Bligh's spoken about you. He was in raptures over the island.' She waved a hand in an encompassing arc. 'We've all been dying to see it, but Bligh wanted to come on ahead and get everything in order before we descended on him.'

The same young man set one small and two large suitcases down beside the girl and she smilingly thanked him. 'Oh, I have to get out to Cascade Court and Bligh doesn't know I'm arriving. I want to surprise him. Do you think you could take me?' she appealed.

Kezia's mind was reeling. This had to be some crazy tormenting nightmare. Here was Devereaux's wife, proof of his duplicity, admitting that her husband had spoken to her about Kezia. It was unbelievable.

The smile on Dale's face faltered a little when Kezia remained silent and she drew herself into some semblance of order. 'Well, I already have a fare, but . . .'

The other girl's face fell. 'Oh, I see. Is there another taxi?'

The last one had left as Kezia was stowing the suitcases in her boot. 'No, they've all gone. But I guess I could take you if you don't mind sharing.'

'Oh, no, I don't mind at all.' Dale eagerly picked up one of her suitcases and juggled her large shoulder bag.

'I'll take the two large ones if you can manage the small one and my parcel,' said Kezia, and led the way out to the taxi, her heart beginning to renew its aching with a vengeance. Dale Devereaux was a nice young woman and Bligh Devereaux was . . .

'I've been really looking forward to joining Bligh and maybe helping him out with the motel,' the other girl remarked as they walked across the parking area. 'I wasn't supposed to be arriving for another few weeks, but,' she shrugged as she put the suitcase down beside the car, 'I've had a bout of man trouble that's been dying a lingering death for months. To cut a long story short, Roger and I decided to call it quits, and so here I am falling on Bligh's doorstep. He'll be a darling as usual and let me weep all over his shirt front for the umpteenth time. I don't know what I'd do without him.'

Kezia set one suitcase into the boot and arranged the other two so that the extra ones would fit in. What sort of marriage did these two have? They appeared to go their own ways, do their own thing quite mutually. Didn't he care that his wife had been involved with another man? Was that why he thought nothing of starting an affair with her? Tears welled in her eyes and she fought them back as she climbed behind the wheel of the taxi and introduced her three passengers.

Somehow she managed to concentrate on the mechanics of driving the car, chatting to the two middle-aged women in the back seat and the young one beside her, pointing out various landmarks, listening to them discussing their trepidation at the size of the small Norfolk Island Airlines Beechcraft that had borne them to the island.

In no time at all the other two women had been deposited at their hotel and then Kezia was alone again with Dale Devereaux.

'It's just as Bligh described it,' Dale was gazing about her with interest. 'The island looked like some sort of paradise from the air as we approached.'

'It does seem to appear out of nowhere, doesn't it?' Kezia drove slowly through the shopping centre, waiting for an ancient utility that pulled out from the Swiss House.

'What sort of motel is Cascade Court?' asked Dale. 'I mean, I saw the photos of it, but Bligh said it needed a lot of remodelling.'

'It's one of the best resorts on the island.' Kezia only just managed to keep the bite out of her voice.

'Oh, I gathered that. Nothing but the best for Bligh.' Her laugh robbed her words of any sting. 'He was really enthusiastic about it. I haven't seen him so fired up for years. He's kind of grown pretty cyncial and—well, I guess when you're such a success it dulls a bit after a while, having no more mountains to climb, so to speak.'

Kezia made no comment, her thoughts going relentlessly back to the morning she'd sat with Bligh on the top of Mount Pitt watching the sun rise. That morning he'd climbed a mountain and . . .

'Have you lived here on the island long?' the other girl was asking.

'All my life. Our family came to live here from Pitcairn Island.'

'You mean you're actually a descendant of the mutineers? How wonderful to be part of it! It's a fantastic story. I've read a couple of versions of it. I suppose Bligh told you Dad believes he's related to that Captain William Bligh?'

'Yes, he told me.' Kezia had to suppress a sigh of releif as she turned into Cascade Court. 'We're here.'

The young porter appeared by magic and took the two suitcases Kezia heaved out of the boot.

'Where's Mr Devereaux?' Dale asked him, searching in her bag for some money to pay her fare.

'In his office, madam,' the young man replied, his eyes going to Kezia and back to the new arrival.

'Good. I'll be able to surprise him. Oh, dear, where's my change?' She sifted through what seemed like a multitude of odds and ends in the bottomless bag. 'Can you wait a minute, Kezia? I'll get some from Bligh.'

'No, it's all right—another time will do,' she said hurriedly, not wanting to witness Bligh's reunion with his wife.

'I can't not pay you, Kezia. Ah!' She smiled and drew her purse from her shoulder bag. 'Found!' She began counting out the fare while Kezia stood tensed to make her escape, but she'd left it too late. Her heart sank even as she turned towards the open doors.

His blue eyes flicked over Dale to Kezia and as he caught sight of her he paused in mid-stride, his face actually paling. He continued down the steps and although his expression was now set in impassive lines he was still white about the mouth.

'Bligh!' Dale forgot her purse and threw herself into his arms.

Over her head his blue eyes met Kezia's and she couldn't look away, couldn't seem to get her frozen muscles to work, to carry her from the torment of seeing another woman in his arms.

'I hope you don't mind me arriving a little early?' Dale was saying, laughing confidently up at him.

'No, of course not.' Not for a moment did his eyes waver from Kezia and she felt herself beginning to blush at the vivid intensity in his gaze.

'I don't suppose you're really surprised to see me. You did warn me about Roger,' Dale grimaced. 'You were right again, of course.' She put her arm through his. 'Just once I'd like to prove you wrong, you devil!'

Life began to ebb back into Kezia's numb limbs and she took a step towards the car. Bligh moved forward then, bringing Dale with him. 'Kezia, just a minute.'

He looked a little uncertain, but of course he couldn't be, not Bligh Devereaux. He was always so sure of himself, knew exactly where he was at.

'Have you met, Dale?' he asked, his eyes still harrowing her with the fire in their depths.

'Oh, yes,' Dale smiled easily. 'Kezia and I introduced ourselves at the airport.'

'I ... I'd better be going,' Kezia mumbled dejectedly, and turned to the car. Bligh was there before her to open the door.

'Are you free this evening?' His voice was quiet and he seemed a little breathless. 'To join us, Dale and me, for dinner?'

She stared up at him with disbelieving eyes, wondering that the pain she had already experienced could grow so agonizingly worse.

'No, I'm afraid I can't,' she climbed into the car, 'thank you all the same.' So polite, she jeered herself, when she wanted to scream, cascade her hurt over him.

'Just a minute, Kezia.' Dale waved the notes in her hand. 'You fare. Have you got a dollar, Bligh?'

He pulled out his wallet and handed Dale the money which she took with a smile. 'I knew I could depend on you,' she teased him with her eyes as she handed Kezia the money. 'Isn't he the best brother in the world?'

Kezia let out the clutch in shock and the car jumped forward and stalled indignantly.

'Did you say brother?' she breathed as the other two looked down at her.

'Well, half-brother, actually,' Dale smiled uncertainly, not understanding the reason for Kezia's shocked paleness. 'My mother was our father's second wife.'

'Your brother,' Kezia repeated stupidly. 'Your brother? I thought ... your surnames were the same and . . .' she pulled herself up quickly and dragged her shocked eyes from Bligh's face. 'I have to go,' she said agitatedly, and restarted the engine, driving as though the devil himself pursued her away from the motel and the couple who stared after her in surprise.

Sitting back against the cement paraput, Kezia shoved her hands into the front pockets of her parka, the hood pushed back to let the cool breeze tossle her dark hair. Her brother. He was Dale's brother, not her husband. She could even now almost giggle hysterically. Her brother!

The words had churned around inside her for the rest of the day and all night as she lay wide awake, unable to relax enough to even contemplate sleep. Her brother.

She tried to recall every moment she'd spent with Bligh since her return from Brisbane, trying to re-evaluate his attitude, his words. But she couldn't seem to manage it. For somehow she was afraid to even think, let alone to hope, that perhaps he might care.

He was interested, she told herself. And maybe that was all it was. Just because he might be attracted to her it didn't mean a thing. He still might only be looking to have an affair.

Sighing, she hunched her shoulders, her hands in her pockets holding the front of her parka together over her warm jumper. Soon the sun would be rising over the water to climb Mount Pitt and join her, bringing a new day. And for the first time in her life she wanted to stave off the new dawning, afraid to face what the day may hold.

The car was there before she was even aware of it, for the wind had disguised the sound of its climb up the winding road, but she did catch the closing click of the driver's door and turned her head. It was still relatively dark, but she recognised the shape of him immediately, knowing instinctively every contour of his hard body, and her heart began to race in a wild frenzy of alarm and elation.

He strode easily up the incline to stop beside her and sat down, his hands in the pockets of his dark cord jeans, the thick rollneck of his light sweater defining the firm familiar line of his jaw.

'I hoped I'd find you here,' he said at last, just as the sky began its first lightening.

Tears welled in Kezia's eyes and she gave a shiver of reaction, scarcely daring to breathe in case he should disappear.

'I was sure you would have been on that plane.' His voice was almost expressionless, and he wasn't looking at her, didn't make a move to touch her, although her senses cried out to be gathered into those strong arms. 'What changed your mind?' he asked quietly.

'I never had any intention of going with Shann,' she told him honestly. 'This is my home. No matter where I went I'd have had to come back.' To you, she added in her heart.

'I'm glad you didn't go,' he said simply.

Kezia's heart lurched. Did he mean . . .? How she wished she'd had more experience. She couldn't begin to know what to say, for perhaps he only meant he was glad she hadn't made a fool of herself with Shann. A tear trembled on her eyelashes and her voice caught in her throat, her teeth clenching till they ached.

They sat in silence as the sky began to glow, seemed to take the cold bite out of the sharp breeze. And some of the warmth seeped inside Kezia and she turned her head to look at him. His eyes were on the distant dawning which threw his profile into a distinct relief so achingly familiar to her that his name came out spontaneously in a broken whisper. Bligh turned to face her then, his eyes bleak, a forlornness sitting on the planes of his face. Kezia's heart lurched and she knew she wanted nothing more than to sweep away his sadness. She had to take a chance.

'I thought Dale was your wife.' The words tumbled out almost incoherently. 'I thought you had no right to kiss me the way you did. I thought you were just amusing yourself with me.' She gulped back the tears and her hand reached out to touch his arm. 'I didn't want to be part of a cheap affair.'

His eyes seemed to devour her and his hand covered hers where it rested on his arm, the grip of his fingers almost painful. 'Kezia, I would never have asked that of you,' he said thickly, and the vivid blueness of his gaze held her mesmerised with its intensity. 'I've had affairs before, but nothing, no one has ever come close to the way I feel about you, my love.'

A great weight was lifted from her heart and his name was a cry on her lips seconds before he pulled her into his arms, his hands sliding under her parka, his lips capturing hers in gentle adoration as he strove to control the desire she felt burn through his body. He lifted his head to look down at her, the crush of his arms confirming the extent of his arousal.

'I love you more than life itself, Kezia McCoy,' he told her raggedly. 'I wanted to tell you the morning we sat here watching that other sunrise, but I thought I'd be rushing you, that it was too soon.'

His words, the depth of feeling in the timbre of his voice, flowed about her, lifting her upwards until she thought surely the whole world had stopped spinning.

He drew a deep breath. 'And then after Evans' farewell party I thought I'd left it too late.'

'Oh, Bligh, I love you, too. When you went without a word after we'd watched the sunrise I ...' she began.

'Without word? But I left a message for you at reception,' he broke in. 'You didn't receive it?'

Kezia shook her head. 'No. There was nothing.'

He frowned. 'Kez, I'm sorry. I naturally assumed that Raewyn would tell you. Was that why you wouldn't talk to me in Brisbane?'

'Partly. And Dale, of course. It's been such an agony thinking you weren't free. I couldn't bear the thought of facing life without you.'

'There's no way you'll get the chance to do that, my love,' he stated with his old arrogance. 'Now that I have you unresisting in my arms I'll never let you go.'

As he smiled down at her the sun broke over the water to paint the sky with the fiery glow of a newborn day, a fresh beginning.

'How on earth did you come to imagine Dale was my wife?' he asked, his fingers moving sensuously over her back to slide beneath the warmth of her jumper.

Kezia moved responsively closer. 'I phoned your house in Brisbane and Dale answered. When she said she was Dale Devereaux I just assumed she had to be your wife. Perhaps I was over prepared to expect the worst, and she was with you at the auction. Everything added up. After the night of Shann's party,' Kezia's eyes fell from his and his lips twitched in a teasing smile, 'when Dale turned up at the airport I felt so cheap and angry with myself, I could barely look her in the eye.'

'And when I walked out to see you standing there by your taxi, here on the island and not off with Shann Evans, I'm afraid I didn't exactly give Dale the welcome she could have expected.' His hand came up to cup her cheek. 'I felt as if someone had pulled the floor out from under me.'

'You did look a little pale.' Kezia turned her lips to kiss the palm of his hand.

'As pale as you did when Dale told you I was only her brother?' he asked, and drew her closer into his arms. 'Oh, Kezia, I've loved you from the first moment I set eyes on you, all wrapped up in a pair of outsized overalls with dirt smudges on that beautiful nose.' His lips gently kissed her nose. 'Even though I wondered just what kind of virago I'd discovered. Wielding spanners and deciding all manner of punishment for your poor unsuspecting brother!'

'Oh, yes? Any punishment meted out to my poor unsuspecting brother was more than justifiable, believe me,' she laughed, snuggling into the solid warmth of his chest. 'My mother thought you were the handsomest mainlander she'd seen.' Kezia chuckled, running a gently teasing fingertip lightly over his nose, to linger on his lips.

'Your mother has impeccable taste. Just like her beautiful daughter.' Bligh's gaze settled on her smiling mouth and she saw the flame in the depths of his eyes leap into a thousand all-consuming sparks before his lips came down to possess hers with desperate desire, and she closed her eyes, giving herself up to the ecstasy of his kisses.

'Oh, Kezia, do you realise just what you do to me?' he asked raggedly, his heart racing beneath her hands. 'I've always prided myself on my self-assurance,' he grimaced, 'but this hard-headed businessman goes completely to pieces simply thinking about you!'

She pressed her lips into the curve of his neck, her fingers moving in the thickness of his hair.

'And to think I almost lost you!' A shudder passed over him and Kezia held him close. 'When I heard that damn plane fly over I . . .' He shook his head. 'I've never felt such impotent rage. It was any agony far beyond any physical pain. All I could do was stand there helplessly and curse myself for a bloody fool.'

'I was sorry the moment I let you think I was going with Shann,' Kezia admitted. 'I don't know why I did it. Perhaps I thought you might suffer a little of my hurt.'

'Now that I did,' he said with feeling. 'Where you were concerned, Kez, I couldn't seem to get anything right, doing the wrong thing, saying the wrong thing. I couldn't even stop myself criticising Shann Evans, even when I knew it upset you. The truth was I was plain dead green with jealousy of his hold on your heart.'

'There was not need. I realised almost from the moment I met you that I never loved Shann, not the way I love you.' She smiled wryly. 'I'd known him all my life and had him woven in a crazy dream world all mixed up with our heritage, a continuance of our life on the island, our own nationality, if you like. I couldn't see past that. I only saw in Shann what I wanted to see. Until you came along and held my flimsy dream world up to the light of reality and forced me to see its failings. I suppose I resented that. It made me feel young and foolish, so inexperienced I couldn't hope to keep your interest. So I allowed that resentment to discolour everything you did—with Shann, with the island, and the motel.'

'I never aimed to antagonise you for the sake of it Kezia. Anything I changed in the motel I changed as a businessman. There was nothing personal in it. And it was never my intention to give you the impression that I was stealing a part of your island. I wanted the chance to share your haven, not ridicule your heritage, but become a part of it! If you'll let me.' His eyes held hers. 'Well, Kezia McCoy, could you see your way clear to marrying a mere mainlander and a descendant, as yet unproven, of Captain Bligh, to boot?'

She nodded without hesitation, her eyes bright with tears. 'I'd be honoured,' she said radiantly, and heard him catch his breath.

'Let's make it soon.' He held her fiercely close. 'As soon as we legally can.'

They looked at each other and laughed as though they shared the very best secret in the world, sitting back together holding hands, watching the sun bringing the island to life.

'This has always been my favourite spot,' Kezia sighed happily. 'Perhaps I knew that I would find you here in my very special place.'

'The closest place to heaven, didn't you call it?' He lifted her hand to his lips and kissed it. 'There could be no place more special for both of us.' He sat up. 'Kezia, why don't we have the ceremony up here? What could be more fitting, getting married right here on the top of our world?'

And so they were. On a bright sunkissed morning, with a police car escorting them to the top of Mount Pitt and their families and friends gathered around them in a group that made Kezia think that the entire island had turned out for their wedding day.

But then Bligh was smiling at her with his love reflected in his blue eyes and everything else was relegated to the background, even her beloved island, for that smile to Kezia was a heart-stopping breath of paradise, the closest place to heaven here on earth.

Romance on your holiday

Wherever you go, you can take Mills & Boon romance with you. Mills & Boon Holiday Reading Pack, published on June 10th in the UK, contains four new Mills & Boon paperback romances, in an easy-to-pack presentation case.

Carole Mortimer	— LOVE UNSPOKEN
Penny Jordan	— RESCUE OPERATION
Elizabeth Oldfield	— DREAM HERO
Jeneth Murrey	— FORSAKING ALL OTHER

On sale where you buy paperbacks. £3.80 (UK net)

Mills & Boon
The rose of romance

ROMANCE

ROMANCE

Next month's romances from Mills & Boon

Each month, you can choose from a world of variety in romance with Mills & Boon. These are the new titles to look out for next month.

JILTED Sally Wentworth
HIGHLAND GATHERING Elizabeth Graham
A SUDDEN ENGAGEMENT Penny Jordan
ALL THAT HEAVEN ALLOWS Anne Weale
CAGE OF SHADOWS Anne Mather
THE GUARDED HEART Robyn Donald
LION'S DOMAIN Rosemary Carter
FACE THE TIGER Jane Donnelly
THE TIDES OF SUMMER Sandra Field
NIGHT OF POSSESSION Lilian Peake
PRICE TO BE MET Jessica Steele
NO ROOM IN HIS LIFE Nicola West

Buy them from your usual paperback stockist, or write to: Mills & Boon Reader Service, P.O. Box 236, Thornton Rd, Croydon, Surrey CR9 3RU, England. Readers in South Africa-write to: Mills & Boon Reader Service of Southern Africa, Private Bag X3010, Randburg, 2125.

Mills & Boon
the rose of romance

How to join in a whole new world of romance

It's very easy to subscribe to the Mills & Boon Reader Service. As a regular reader, you can enjoy a whole range of special benefits. Bargain offers. Big cash savings. Your own free Reader Service newsletter, packed with knitting patterns, recipes, competitions, and exclusive book offers.

We send you the very latest titles each month, postage and packing free – no hidden extra charges. There's absolutely no commitment – you receive books for only as long as you want.

We'll send you details. Simply send the coupon – or drop us a line for details about the Mills & Boon Reader Service Subscription Scheme.
Post to: Mills & Boon Reader Service, P.O. Box 236, Thornton Road, Croydon, Surrey CR9 3RU, England.
*Please note: READERS IN SOUTH AFRICA please write to: Mills & Boon Reader Service of Southern Africa, Private Bag X3010, Randburg 2125, S. Africa.

Please send me details of the Mills & Boon Subscription Scheme.
NAME (Mrs/Miss) _____ EP3
ADDRESS _____

_____

COUNTY/COUNTRY_____ POST/ZIP CODE_____
BLOCK LETTERS, PLEASE

Mills & Boon
the rose of romance